D1049655

# MISADVENTURES

## WITH A

# SUPER HERO

BY
ANGEL PAYNE

# MISADVENTURES

## WITH A

# SUPER HERO

BY
ANGEL PAYNE

WATERHOUSE PRESS

This book is an original publication of Waterhouse Press.

This is a work of fiction. Names, characters, places, and incidents either are the product of the author's imagination or are used fictitiously, and any resemblance to actual persons, living or dead, business establishments, events, or locales is entirely coincidental. The publisher does not assume any responsibility for third-party websites or their content.

Copyright © 2017 Waterhouse Press, LLC
Cover Design by Waterhouse Press.
Cover images: Shutterstock

All Rights Reserved.
No part of this book may be reproduced, scanned, or distributed in any printed or electronic format without permission. Please do not participate in or encourage piracy of copyrighted materials in violation of the author's rights. Purchase only authorized editions.

PRINTED IN THE UNITED STATES OF AMERICA

ISBN: 978-1-943893-44-7

*For Thomas...my incredible super hero, every single day.*

# PROLOGUE

## REECE

She's got the body of a goddess, the eyes of a temptress, and the lips of a she-devil.

And tonight, she's all mine. In every way I can possibly fantasize. And fuck, do I have a lot of fantasies.

Riveted by her seductive glance, I follow her into the waiting limo. A couple of friends from the party we've just left—their names already as blurry as the lights of Barcelona's Plaça Reial—swing hearty waves of departure, as if Angelique La Salle is taking me away on a six-month cruise to paradise.

*Ohhh, yeah.*

I've never been on a cruise. As an heir to a massive hotel dynasty, I've never wanted for the utmost in luxurious destinations, but I've never been on a cruise. I think I'd like it. Nothing to think about but the horizon...and booze. Freedom from reporters, like the mob that were flashing their cameras in my face back at the club.

What'll the headlines be, I wonder.

Undoubtedly, they've already got a few combinations composed—a mix of the buzz words already trending about me this week.

*Party Boy. Player. The Heir with the Hair. The Billionaire with the Bulge.*

Well. Mustn't disappoint them about the bulge.

And I sure as fuck don't plan to.

If my brain just happens to enjoy this as much as my body...I sure as hell won't complain.

Maybe she'll be the one.

Maybe she'll be...more.

The one who'll change things...at last.

As the driver merges the car into Saturday night traffic, Angelique moves her lush green gaze over everything south of my neck. Within five seconds my body responds. The fantasies in my brain are overcome by the depraved tempest of my body. My chest still burns from the five girls on the dance floor who group-hickied me. My shoulders are on fire from the sixth girl who clawed me like a madwoman while watching from behind. My dick pulses from a hard-on that won't stop because of the seventh girl—and the line of coke she snorted off it.

Angelique gazes at that part with lingering appreciation.

*"C'est magnifique."* Her voice is husky as she closes in, sliding a hand into the open neckline of my shirt. Where's my tie? I was wearing one tonight—at some point. The Prada silk is long gone, much like my self-control. Beneath her roaming fingers, my skin shivers and then heats.

Well...shit.

Even if she's not going to be the one, she is at least *someone*. A body to warm the night. A presence, of *any* kind, to fill the depths.

The emptiness I stopped thinking about a long damn time ago.

"You're magnificent too," I murmur, struggling to maintain control as she swings a Gumby-loose limb over my lap and straddles me. What little there is of her green cocktail dress rides up her thighs. She's wearing nothing underneath, of course—a fact that should have my cock much happier than it is. Troubling...but not disturbing. I'm hard, just not throbbing. Not *needing*. I'm not sure what I need anymore, only that I seem to spend a lot of time searching for it.

"So flawless," she croons, freeing the buttons of my shirt down to my waist. "*Oui*. These shoulders, so broad. This stomach, so etched. You are perfect, *mon chéri*. So perfect for this."

"For what?"

"You shall see. Very soon."

"I don't even get a hint?" I spread a smile into the valley between her breasts.

"That would take the fun out of the surprise, *n'est-ce pas*?"

I growl but don't push the point, mostly because she makes the wait well worth it. During the drive, she taunts and tugs, strokes and licks, teases and entices, everywhere and anywhere, until I'm damn near tempted to order the driver to pull over so I can pull out a condom and screw this temptress right here and now.

But where the hell is here?

Almost to the second I think the question, the limo pulls into an industrial park of some sort. A secure one, judging by the high walls and the rolling door that allows us to roll directly into the building.

Inside, at least in the carport, all is silent. The air smells like cleaning chemicals and leather...and danger. Nothing like a hint of mystery to make a sex club experience all the sweeter.

"A little trip down memory lane, hmmm?" I nibble the bottom curve of Angelique's chin. It's been three weeks since we'd met in a more intimate version of this type of place, back in Paris. I'd been hard-up. She'd been alluring. End of story. Or beginning, depending on how one looks at it. "How nostalgic of you, darling."

As she climbs from the limo, she leaves her dress behind in a puddle on the ground. It wasn't doing much good where I bunched it around her waist anyway. "Come, my perfect Adonis."

*Perfect.* I don't hear that word often, at least not referring to me. Too often, I'm labeled with one of those media favorites, or if I'm lucky, one of the specialties cooked up by Dad or Chase in their weekly phone messages. Dad's a little more lenient, going for shit like "hey, stranger" or "my gypsy kid." Chase doesn't pull so many punches. Lately, his favorite has been "Captain Fuck-Up."

"Bet *you'd* like to be Captain Fuck-Up right about now, asshole," I mutter as two gorgeous women move toward me, summoned by a flick of Angelique's fingers. Their white lab coats barely hide their generous curves, and I find myself taking peeks at their sheer white hose, certain the things must be held up by garters. Despite the kinky getups, neither of them crack so much as a smile while they work in tandem to strip me.

I'm so caught up in what the fembots are doing, I've missed Angelique putting on a new outfit. Instead of the gold stilettos she'd rocked at the club, she's now in sturdier heels and a lab coat. Her blonde waves are pulled up and pinned back.

"Well, well, well. Doctor La Salle, I presume?" Eyeing her new attire with a wicked smirk, I ignore the sudden twist in my gut as she sweeps a stare over me. Her expression is stripped of lust. She's damn near clinical.

"Oh, I am not a doctor, *chéri*."

I arch my brows and put both hands on my hips, strategically guiding her sights back to my jutting dick. I may not know how the woman likes her morning eggs yet, but I *do* know she's a sucker for an arrogant bastard—especially when he's naked, erect, and not afraid to do something about it.

"Well, that's okay, *chérie*." I swagger forward. "I can pretend if you can."

Angelique draws in a long breath and straightens. Funny, but she's never looked hotter to me. Even now, when she really does look like a doctor about to lay me out with shitty test results. "No more pretending, *mon ami*."

"No more—" My stomach twists again. I glance backward. The two assistants aren't there anymore, unless they've magically transformed into two of the burliest hulks I've ever seen not working a nightclub VIP section.

But these wonder twins clearly aren't here to protect me.

In tandem, they pull me back and flatten me onto a rolling gurney.

And buckle me down. Tight.

Really tight.

"What. The. *Fuck*?"

"Sssshhh." She's leaning over my face—the wonder fuckers have bolted my head in too—brushing tapered fingers across my knitted forehead. "This will be easier if you don't resist, *mon trésor*."

"This? This...*what*?"

Her eyes blaze intensely before glazing over—with insanity.

"History, Reece! We are making *history,* and you are now part of it. One of the most integral parts!"

"You're—you're batshit. You're not forging history, you bitch. You're committing a crime. This is kidnapping!"

Her smile is full of eerie serenity. "Not if nobody knows about it."

"People are going to know if I disappear, Angelique."

"Who says you are going to disappear?"

For some reason, I have no comeback for that. No. I *do* know the reason. Whatever she's doing here might be insanity—but it's well-planned insanity.

Which means...

I'm screwed.

The angel I trusted to take me to heaven has instead handed me a pass to hell.

Making this, undoubtedly, the hugest mess my cock has ever gotten me into.

# CHAPTER ONE

## EMMA

*One year later...*

The executive offices at Hotel Brocade are always a fun place to be, but they're even more exciting when the boys in the reservations bay are trying to kill each other.

"Bam!"

"Kazow!"

"You're dead."

"Not if you're dead first."

"Yeah, right. Because your spleen on the ground isn't an indication I got you first, huh, crap-for-brains?"

Ahhhh. Nothing like the sounds of cybergeeks in full slay-or-be-slain mode, a special perk of working the six p.m. to four a.m. shift. When splattered spleens are invoked, I know it's time to finish up my break and get back to work. Let nobody say the new girl didn't learn the important lessons fast.

Thank God.

Because I really need this job.

I swore I'd cut off my right nipple if I got this position. The left one too, though thankfully things never came to that. I intend to keep my nipples *and* the job by being the hardest-working person in the building.

This job is what finally got me out of hell.

Okay, Orange County hasn't always been hell. It just took a dive that direction once Dad got his massive promotion to VP at an international conglomerate with a massive campus in Irvine, thrusting our family into another income bracket—and the stratosphere of vanilla-flavored snobbery.

A.k.a. Hell.

But I've escaped. I'm no longer part of that world. I've finally begun a life filled with more than hair appointments, yoga classes, and fretting about the carb count in my morning muffin.

I intend to stay here.

This job is the key to truly beginning my life.

I arrive back at my office, a proud smile erupting as I take in my view. Twinkle lights glow in the olive and palm trees surrounding the pool area. Banks of tropical flowers flutter in the gauzy night breeze. A few people are enjoying the hot tub across the deck, quietly laughing and talking, but there's nobody in the bigger pool, so the water is reflected as lazy aqua swirls against my office window. The scene is stunning, even at night.

God, I *really* love working here.

"Well, good evening, Miss Emmalina Crist."

I smile toward the source of the greeting issued in a musical accent from my office doorway.

"Good evening to you too, Miss Neeta Jain."

Neeta folds her arms and grins. "The warriors of Geekdom have you cutting and running for the sane side of the building again?"

I laugh, slightly nervously. Neeta is dressed nearly the same as me, in a dark skirt suit with a satin blouse beneath, but on her the look is sleek and glam, while I feel like the girl playacting at adulting. Which is ridiculous. I'm nearly twenty-four now. I landed this job on my own. Paid for this suit with my own money. It's not dress up. It's mine. This *life* is mine.

*I can do this. I can do this. I can do this.*

I intend to keep repeating it, in my heart and on my lips, until I really believe it.

For now, I push aside how her waterfall of dark hair and perfectly kohled eyes remind me of the pretty but plain world for which I still feel like the poster child.

"It's all right," I assure her. "Wade and Fershan deliver when it matters most. Their guest-satisfaction scores are among the highest for the Reservations Department. As long as they're Prince Charmings for the public, I don't care if they eviscerate each other a hundred times tonight."

She laughs softly while walking toward the window. "Excellent point." But her composure jolts the second she pivots toward my monitor. "And speaking of excellent points..." Her jaw goes slack. She drops into my chair. "Look at the glory of *this* one."

I move behind her, curious about what's caused her to gawk. Every staff computer is programmed to boot up into the guest room online menu, so we stay aware of any technical issues. In addition to local attractions, there's a live feed of local news features cultivated for the maximum relevance to our guests, though the feature is often more valuable for us. Our downtown location puts us in the thick of it during major emergencies—which could be anything from a six-plus magnitude earthquake to a diva breaking a fingernail en route to an awards show—so the constantly changing feed has become an essential compass.

Right now, Neeta expands the compass with eager swiftness. I won't be surprised if her throaty gasps and dreamy sighs develop into drooling.

"Glory?" I mean every note of my fascinated echo. I need to see what's turned her from worldly and sleek to stuttering and adolescent.

Once I step around and view the screen, a frown takes over. "A convenience store robbery?" I thought I'd be helping her ogle the hottest hunks on some movie premiere red carpet. "Okay, even the OC peasant isn't getting the appeal." I wonder if we need to change the feed to another station. Last time I checked, stories like this didn't fit *any* of the Richards Resorts "R's of Hospitality." *Relax. Revitalize. Renew.*

"A *thwarted* convenience store robbery." Neeta jabs a red-tipped fingernail in emphasis. "And look at the god who did the thwarting."

"God?"

"God."

I peer closer at the feed. It shows the same basic news-chopper view of the little store, like so many others in the city. Semi-busy street intersection. Palm trees. Geraniums planted in the median. Couple of parking spaces and a bike rack out front. Posters for beer and lottery tickets in the front window. Neon sign. *Yes, We're Open.* There's nothing special about the police presence, either. A pair of cruisers with lights flashing, turning the area into an ironic urban disco.

"I really...don't see what's so..."

But then I *do* see.

The screen changes, showing cell phone footage timestamped from forty-five minutes ago. Looks like amateur stuff captured from across the street from the store. The cell owner's commentary can be heard, captured along with the images.

"Damn. What assholes would rob Santa Claus?"

Sure enough, the store's proprietor is a sweet old guy who probably volunteers as Saint Nick around the holidays. I wouldn't believe any less, though right now he stands behind the counter wearing a *Go Dodgers* T-shirt. Though the leader of the hoodlums has drawn a gun, the man reaches for them like Santa trying to reason with a pair of Jack Frosts with matching bleached Mohawks.

"That sweet man," Neeta murmurs. "I'd be on the floor in a puddle of terror."

"You mean like her?"

The cell phone shot pans wider to include a woman no older than us cowering on the floor. Bad guy number three, just noticing her, stomps over for the grab.

But he clutches at nothing but air because the woman has... levitated.

At least five feet. Straight into the air.

"What...the..."

"Right?" Neeta gasps as the girl starts to scream. "That's not even the best part."

"There's *more*?"

I barely get the words out before the poor woman starts to

gently float toward the back of the store as if being carried by some invisible divinity. There's five feet of empty air between her and the floor, and a discernible black line scorching the linoleum, marking the terrified woman's path to safety.

"How...is...that...?"

"Right?" Neeta repeats.

"No," I blurt. "*Not* right. How the hell is that even possible?"

"They say he does it with massive electric fields," Neeta responds. "Though how *that* works is still anyone's guess."

"He who?"

"He...him." She declares it as if heralding Eros himself, just as another man appears at the left of the video. That's barely an exaggeration. The figure to which she's referring could double as the god in a movie. He seems to appear from nowhere, as ceiling lights burst and shower behind him, like he's descending from freaking Mount Olympus in a fit of rage. Damn good way to describe what the guy's mood looks like too. His strides are wide. His arms are an A, framing the air on either side of his body. His fists look like brutal coils at the end of muscled ropes. And holy shit, do I mean muscled. Having a tennis star for a sister means I actually know the name of every striation in the human arm, though rarely am I able to recall them while *looking* at them. His legs present the same fun game, and don't get me started on his abdominals.

On second thought, go ahead and get me started.

All of that is encased in an outfit I can only describe as motocross meets rock god. The black leathers are so tight he should look like a pretentious jackass but weirdly doesn't. His get-up has flexible fabric insets of some sort which cushion his glorious body in all the key places he needs to move. He even wears kick-ass boots—if that's what they can be called—evoking Black Ops or SEALs, pieced in a crisscross up to his knees.

He's part ninja, part ultimate fighter, part thundercloud—and a hundred percent captivating.

I can't rip my stare off him. He seems to uncoil power like a live electrical wire—but with an insane body.

*Truly* insane.

"Holy...shit." I finally summon the bandwidth in my brain to breathe.

"Nothing holy about what I'd love to do that guy." Neeta snorts. "Whoever he is."

"What do you—"

Eros-ninja-thunder-dude interrupts my question, stalking toward the robbers and planting his feet the same width as his fists. He lowers his head as if he's saying something, and it earns him a triple hoodlum rush—which he answers by raising both fists and spreading his fingers until they're strained wide. In another universe, I'd expect spider webs or fireballs to fly from his palms. In this one, there's only a tangible but invisible shudder through the air that acts like a three-way punch striking the robbers.

It's as impossible to comprehend as the levitation trick on the woman, but it's the truth. Neeta's gasp, in tandem with mine, tells me she thoroughly agrees. We're riveted as the hero lifts his arm a little higher and flings it as if throwing trash away—which is very likely what he's thinking too—as the hoodlums scatter into the air like a wind-tossed trio of used slushy cups, flying twenty feet before crashing into the drink coolers at the back of the store. They stick there for a few seconds, bawling in terror, before plummeting along with the glass to the floor. Whoever's taking the cell footage provides a perfect flash of commentary.

"Yeah! Dude is takin' care of business!"

I'm faintly aware Wade has scooped up his cyberguts long enough to wander in our direction. At the sounds of our reactions to the video, he scoots in behind us. "Fersh!" he shouts. "Get over here. It's him."

"Sure as hell is." Every syllable out of Neeta is just sultry.

"Him who?" I demand as Fershan dips his head, baring a smile that's brilliant against his dark skin.

"Dude," he repeats, shoving Wade's bony shoulder. "You're right!"

"Him *who*?"

"Nobody knows," Neeta supplies.

I glance back at the monitor. "Wait. Are you serious?" My scowl becomes a gape. "Is *he* serious? Is he really wearing a mask?"

Okay, not a big one. It's like the Maserati of masks. Sleek and black and subtle, fitted like a tight blindfold across his upper face but with eyeholes. I can't tell a lot from the angle of the video, but the eyeholes look like rectangles, almost making him look like a wavy-haired hipster with designer glasses. But instead of skinny jeans and a cardigan, he rocks custom leathers and weird-but-hot ninja boots.

"I think he's pretty serious," Wade responds as the ninja thunder god pivots, grabs a couple of extension cords off an endcap, and makes his way to the back of the store. Next to the hanging cords is a rack of mini flashlights, which all start to blink as his hand passes near.

"What on..." I whip a startled glance at the guys. "Did you see—"

"Yep," they answer in unison.

For the next thirty seconds, we only see the storeowner glancing furtively toward the spot where weird electro man flung the bad guys, though the cell phone owner illuminates with his play-by-play. "Boss is usin' those cords to tie those slimebags down. Yeah, man. That's the way."

When the video feed is filled with red and blue lights, the man in the Maserati mask snaps up. At once, hunk-god rapidly strides toward the front of the shop like a man on his way to save the world. Which, at this exact moment, doesn't seem like an exaggeration at all.

Despite his near blur of speed, he's mesmerizing. When he's in the shot, my sights focus on him alone. I'm nervous but attracted, almost feeling like I'm on a first date—pretty lame, considering I haven't exactly logged a ton of those—but the symptoms are the same.

I'm sweating.

I'm throbbing.

I'm aching.

In all the worst places.

"Holy...wow."

The reaction tumbles out before I can stop myself.

"Aha. OC finally figures it out." Neeta's sarcasm saves me from having to summon a fun comeback to Wade and Fershan's shouts.

"Is he gonna do it?"

"C'moooon. He has to do it!"

"Do what?" I ask.

*"Please,"* Neeta drawls. "He's totally going to do it."

"Do *what*?"

The guys bellow in victory as the hero on the screen checks on Santa Claus, spins away from the counter, drops into a stance similar to a competitive runner on the starting block...

And disappears.

"What...the..."

The store fills with flying paper, slushy straws, and condom packets—in short, anything that can easily be tossed around in a strong wind.

A revelation sets in. He didn't disappear. He just left so fast, that was what it looked like.

Fershan and Wade launch into a leaping high five. "Gotta bolt!"

I want to join Neeta in chuckling at them but am trapped in stunned mode. I do manage to blurt, "Excuse me?"

Excitement adds to the ruddy flush on Wade's face. "It's his whoop."

"His whoop?" I echo both syllables with slow caution.

"Like his war cry," Fershan interjects. "It distinguishes him. Puts his unique stamp on shit."

"Because that outfit and the mask don't do that already?"

"Easily copied," Fershan asserts. "But the whoop is unique. Nobody can say it like the original." His gaze twinkles. "Every self-respecting super hero has one."

My scowl disappears—to make room for my gape.

"Okay, whoa. Are you guys telling me—"

A shrill bell cuts me short. The door to our offices, locked at night, sets off the sound when someone uses a fob to open it. The security measure isn't all that safe, though, because most of the time we ignore the alert. The only people who have fobs are supposed to have them.

Tonight, that's not the case.

Wade, Fershan, and Neeta snap their heads up in matching alarm. Before I can question their paranoia, they're hustling like someone's just yanked the fire alarms on every floor of the tower.

"Damn it," Neeta hisses.

The guys add earthier expressions.

"Hey." I sprint as fast as my heels will allow, catching up with them. "What's going on? Somebody want to fill in the new kid?"

"Shit," Wade blurts as if I haven't spoken. He darts a frantic look at his buddy. "He never uses this entrance."

"He who?"

Fershan swallows. "Unless he's spying on us."

"He *who*?" They'll have to acknowledge me eventually.

Neeta rolls her eyes. "His last name is on the letterhead, guys. He's not 'spying.' He's checking up on the business."

I stop so hard my toes turn to jammed stubs in my pumps. *His last name. On the letterhead.* "Holy crap."

My stunned gasp has justifiable cause. The only person I'd never expected to meet, even if I worked days instead of nights, is the same man who approves my paycheck every two weeks. I've heard enough about Reece Richards to figure that much out and to use it as the springboard for my discomfort now.

Okay, yeah, I'd known about the guy before landing the job—though only through thirty-second mentions on glossy entertainment news shows and his paparazzi-favored face on every magazine in the grocery store. The Richards family's gorgeous youngest, known as much for his unconventional business ideas as for his unrestrained sex drive, had only gotten wilder after college. At some point, he stepped into some shit pile so deep, he was banished here, ordered to run the family's West Coast hotels from LA.

Needless to say, I don't expect to meet a happy guy.

Honestly, I wonder if I can get out of meeting him at all. I won't even have to lie about the stack of work I just left behind—and the fact that the news feed is still running on the monitor doesn't hurt either.

Who the hell am I kidding?

All I can think about is watching that robbery footage again. If my rampaging libido doesn't already dictate it, Wade and Fershan's insane claim sure as hell does.

*Super hero?*

They're joking.

They have to be.

Even if the man can toss electric pulses, levitate people, and go zero to light speed in three seconds, that doesn't make him a freaking super hero.

Then what *does* it make him?

I'm forced—saved?—from contemplating that further as the air shimmers with new energy.

Okay, *energy* might be pushing it—but I'm not sure what other label fits this crazy surge of feeling. Is it a quickening? Full-blown anxiety? Leftover thrills from the excitement of watching Maserati Man? This feels like more. As if every ion in the air has been plugged into a cosmic supercharger.

"Mr. Richards. What a pleasant surprise!"

Higher.

Power.

Neither word does him justice. Even strung together, they barely do the job.

Reece Richards is nothing I expected.

And everything I need to fear.

It's not just the physical stuff—though, holy wow, that's the obvious place to start. It's all there, just as I remember from the magazines. The gray gaze so deeply set, the irises resemble midnight. The nose so bold and masculine, it could only be paired with a lush, elegant mouth. And those plush curves are set into a jaw of such sharp angles, I wonder if it's as alluring when clenched. That's all before getting started on his hair. And yes, his hair is really worth the attention. I know this because no matter what, I've always gawked twice at the man's photos just because of those dark auburn waves.

But like I said...that's only the beginning.

His beauty—there really is no other way to say it—is the thinnest nick on the surface of what it's like to look at him. Experience him. Is the air buzzing? Are my breaths xylophoning my ribs? Have my nerve endings been punched to a higher resonance?

*Presence. Aura. Mystique.*

All words I've heard before—and thought I understood.

And never have. Not really.

And that leads back to the wanting. And the fear because of the wanting. As in, already fighting visions of what it'd be like to leap at the man, wrap my thighs around his toned hips, and fit every inch of my needy cleft along his swollen—

"Miss Jain. Good evening."

His acknowledgement to Neeta, followed by similar greetings to the guys, is delivered in a voice as powerful but silken as an ocean wave on the shore. *His voice.* At once it worsens—and heightens—my fantasy. Now, as I mentally jump him, he's rasping like that in my ear. Saying illicit, erotic things... Things I haven't allowed myself to think of doing with a man in a very long time.

*Ride me harder, Emma.*

Things I can't—I won't—allow myself to think now.

*I want to be inside you, Emma.*

Not. Now.

*I'm going to fuck you deep, Emma.*

Not with a man like him.

But all I can focus on *is* him, standing there with his tall, graceful body filling out that dark navy suit and matching tie, the fit so perfect my stare can't help but wander...

Everywhere.

Yes, even down there.

Oh...wow.

His bold, hard elegance is so *not* a disappointment.

*Stop.*

The dictate echoes through my head in Mother's voice. Appropriate. Too damn much so. What would she think if she were here? And why does this man himself seem to read every nuance of those thoughts as they seize my mind—and be just as tense as me about them?

"Good evening yourself, boss." Wade scoots forward and eagerly pumps Richards's hand. Though Neeta barely masks her horror about the familiarity, the "boss" himself seems mildly amused. "Deciding to slum it with the commoners for a bit tonight?"

A ripple of confusion crosses Richards's brow. "Of course," he says slowly, as if reading Wade's lips and guessing at the meaning.

Neeta, still more rattled than I've ever seen her, pushes out a huff. "Mr. Richards doesn't have time for *slumming it.*" With a look drenched in apology, she clarifies, "He's here to collect the weekly reports, of course. And has extended the honor of doing so in person."

It's difficult to interpret Richards's new expression. Relief? Surprise? Both or neither, the angles of his face are beyond riveting. "Right. The reports." His voice is almost a question, though the words don't seem to match.

He pivots toward me and our eyes lock. I open my mouth, but there's nothing. I wonder if it'll ever be capable of sound again. Especially when he appears to lean closer, as if there's something we should say to each other. How did a blade of lightning find its way through the concrete jungle outside to zero in on my swimming, careening senses?

The room tilts, forcing me to an inescapable conclusion.

The lightning...is him.

I suck in a breath. He does the same. He seems puzzled. Angry. Maybe neither. What's he feeling? Why can't I figure it out? I *need* to figure it out. The need is urgent, pinging harder and harder at me...

What the hell is he doing to me?

No. What *isn't* he doing to me? I feel like my sex drive is jammed into a light socket, and I never want to rip it out again—even when Fershan rushes over, wrecking our moment. "It's not yet eleven, Mr. Richards. We can't have the weeklies ready for you until after midnight."

Neeta backhands his shoulder before turning on the charm for Richards again. "What he means is that we'll get to work on them right away for you, sir. We've tricked the system forward in the past for forecasting, and I'm sure this time—"

"No." The man's interruption is calm but commanding as he realigns his posture. "Midnight's not that far away. Just have someone bring the report to the penthouse when it's ready."

"Of course, Mr. Richards. Enjoy the rest of your evening, Mr.—"

The *whump* of the closing elevator doors serves as her conclusion. After two more seconds to confirm the elevator is really carrying the boss away, Wade and Fershan erupt into brutal snickers.

"'My, what a pleasant surprise, Mr. Richards.'"

"'Your wish is my command, Mr. Richards.'"

She jerks an eyebrow Wade's way. "'Slumming it down here, Mr. Richards?'"

"Hey." He ticks the air with a forefinger. "He laughed!"

Fershan snorted. "As much as a guy like that can laugh."

"A guy like that?" I can't help the accusing edge in my echo.

Wade chuffs. "C'mon, Emma. You know what I'm talking about."

"Not sure I do." I'm able to replace the indictment with confusion—and mean it.

"Of course you do," he counters. "Dude probably bought an airline and banged three flight attendants before breakfast this morning. When that far on top of the world, who needs humor? Laughing is a time burner, you know?"

Neeta smirks. "Perhaps he just knows the value of a good smolder."

"A good smolder?" Wade grunts. "Or a bad brood?"

Their round of laughter isn't the reaction I expected. When I step back, flustered, Neeta gently grabs my shoulder. "It's all right, Emma. You don't have to pretend for us. That you didn't feel it?" she supplies when my frown deepens.

"Seriously?" Wade volleys. "Even a corpse would feel it."

I jerk out of Neeta's hold. "Feel *what*? Honestly, *what* are you guys talking about?"

They fall into silence and exchange glances, as if concurring I've just sprouted a second head. And then Wade breaks it to me gently. "The guy's weird, Emma."

*Yeah. In all the most incredible ways.*

But that isn't how Wade means it. One glance at the color staining up to his light ginger hairline and I know it.

"The last time I checked, 'weird' wasn't a crime."

Fershan smacks a hard facepalm. Neeta exhales with meaning.

"You're saying that right now because he's got you by the hormones." Wade's astoundingly gentle about that one. "And that's all right. He's made of money, manners, and damn good genetics. But once all that wears off, you'll start agreeing with us."

"He's got me by the—" I interrupt myself with a grunting laugh. Is he serious right now? Holy shit. He's serious. They all are. "I may be from the boonies, Wade, but I'm not fourteen. My 'hormones' aren't your business—or anyone else's."

Fershan steps in. "Of course," he mutters. "We weren't implying they were. We've just been here longer, and know the situation better, and ask you to consider all that."

"As you trash-talk your own boss?" I retort.

"As we speak the truth as we know it." He exhales roughly. "You've been here less than a month. We were waiting for you to get more settled in before speaking to you about Mr. Richards's... situation. He's not the person you think he is, Emma."

I flash a sardonic look. "No kidding."

"You must listen to me." He grabs both my shoulders. "He's...not right, Emma. The man the media has glorified isn't the one running this hotel. He's..."

"What?" I'm tired of feeling like the one kid on the science team who hasn't seen the dissected frog. "What the heck *is* he? Spit it out, Fershan."

He compresses his lips. "He's just...strange, all right?"

"*Arrgghh.*" I toss up both hands and whirl away from all of them. "No," I finally snap. "It's not all right."

An hour later, I don't feel any differently. If anything, my feet are planted deeper into that mental sand, mostly because of confusion. How have I perceived things so differently than Neeta, Wade, and Fershan? I've only known them for a couple of weeks, but they've seemed sensible and smart—at least until tonight, with all their talk about a super hero on the streets and a wackadoodle boss in the penthouse. That being said, there's no way to disremember the surreal experience of coming face-to-face with Reece Richards. The charged air and the electric presence, sucking out my breaths and telescoping my vision.

Who's really going nuts here?

And do I want to pass up a chance to find out?

My psyche fires off the question as the printer in the next room starts spewing the weekly reports.

And my whole body answers with three sweeps of decisive action.

One kick. Pump number one is off.

Second kick. Pump number two meets the same fate.

Motion three—a ninja-quiet sprint over to the printer and a surreptitious swipe of the contents in the tray.

Before another minute is up, I'm in the back-of-house elevator, jamming my shoes back on and stabbing the button marked P.

Preparing myself for weird.

No. Hoping for it.

# CHAPTER TWO

## REECE

"You've raised 'idiot' to an art form tonight, haven't you?"

Thank fuck it's a rhetorical question. I'd start to worry if this asshole glaring back at me from the penthouse's dark glass had anything to contribute to the conversation. I'm not in the mood to talk, anyway—not even to my own reflection. There are bigger things to worry about.

Much bigger.

As if the point needs clarification, my cock punches against my pants. Right on cue, for the hundredth time in the last hour. Or is it the two hundredth? Does the answer matter? As the residual electricity in my system keeps recirculating through my blood, the torture becomes sheer hell.

I grip the armrests of my desk chair and rear my hips, seeking relief from the ache. No use. I'm as hard as a bull and ready to screw my fucking pen cup. But that'll bring ten point five seconds of relief before the torture surges again, twice as hot and three times as painful. The pen cup probably wouldn't ever speak to me again either.

And *there's* Karma's bitch-slap of the day. Because she can't let *any* day go by without getting that tidbit of a reminder in, can she?

*I deserve this.*

No matter how many Santa Claus shop owners I save between now and my deathbed, it'll be the same.

*I deserve this.*

Exactly *why* did I have to grow a conscience? This new asshole I've transformed into is way more trouble than the old one. Especially when my idiot factor is added into the equation and I choose to go saving Santa's slushies the same night the weekly reports have to be reviewed.

I just pray to God, or whatever deity is choosing to listen to me these days, Neeta doesn't let the new girl bring them up.

Damn. *Damn.*

The new girl.

No. Not a girl. She's a woman, as my traitor of a body reminds me in flashback mode, booting up a vision of her lush curves, white-gold hair, and big aqua eyes in time for my next slam of an erection. I groan, struggling to banish her to my subconscious. I can control that or my hard-on. My system won't allow both.

I opt for keeping my cock in my pants and letting her run wild through my memory.

Her.

*Her who?*

I couldn't get my shit together to even ask her name. Maybe that's a good thing. Because even if I hadn't been battling a thousand extra watts in my bloodstream, what was I supposed to say? *Hi there. I'm Reece. No, you haven't been transported to another planet and had the equilibrium sucked out of your skull. That's just me. Wanna grab sushi sometime?*

The erection starts to subside. "Thank God," I mutter toward the ceiling. "Really, man," I add, taking my first full breath in what feels like days. "I mean it this time."

Finally, I let my hands stretch over the armrests and peer at the veins still throbbing inside them, glowing in some tone between milky white and quicksilver and pulsing in time to my heartbeats, making me look like a goddamned Christmas display. Wouldn't that be the irony of the year? The prodigal son of the Richards clan, invited back for holiday cheer as the Yule tree. *Pass the eggnog, Pops.*

I turn my right arm enough to glance at my watch. Just after midnight. With any luck, there'll be an unexpected hit of calls on the team downstairs, and they'll be too busy with check-ins, pillow requests, and noise complaints to pay attention to the weeklies. This crime-stopper hangover needs another half hour to flush its way completely out of my system. I'm almost there but not close enough.

I force myself to sit up straight. I fish into my desk drawer for the spare elevator keycard. Locking the penthouse against staff elevator access will be as easy as swiping the thing. I only need a few minutes more...

And Karma, with her sick humor, picks that moment to send the damn elevator up.

I throw the card back into the drawer while gritting out the F word. The gears in the elevator shaft whoosh and glide, and eventually the car dings at the landing outside the office.

I take another full breath. It wouldn't be *her*.

After the exercise in awkwardness that was my meeting with

the night crew Scooby Gang earlier, Neeta will make certain it's not. The woman fought hard to add this new one to the team, so she'll want to keep exposure to the Big Bad Wolf to a minimum for now.

Or so I tell myself.

Force myself to believe.

Because believing anything feels a lot like...

Hope.

Hope suddenly fulfilled, with brilliance making me grip the desk once more, as the doors slide open.

And she steps out.

And quickens the air.

And quickens *me*.

Like nothing I've ever experienced before. Like no *one* I've ever met.

So much more than I ever thought possible.

*More.*

No. Goddamnit, that's not possible. Didn't Angelique force-feed me that juicy tidbit clearly enough?

But the woman's presence doesn't let up on the wallop. Literally, my heart rate doubles. The lightning in my blood sizzles before shooting between my thighs, making my ass clench and my hips jerk. It's agony, but it's no longer hell.

It's fucking heaven.

At once, the suspicion hits too. *Don't trust this.* What's wrong with this? I'm not supposed to get heaven. I had my turn at a damn good life and was too huge of an entitled prick to spend a second being grateful for it. I don't get heaven now. Hell's my only reward, and I can only pray it comes sooner than later.

*Don't trust it.*

But as she takes steps closer on those sky-high heels, file folder clutched to her chest and eyes widened as she takes in the suite, I can't help but enjoy her magic. I even savor it. Isn't that what wolves are supposed to do when baby bunnies wander into the lair?

"Hello?" She clears her throat and stops to smooth her jacket and skirt with her free hand, drawing my attention to her graceful curves. Her breasts are high and full, her ass a sweet bump in the skirt. And her legs, especially in those shoes...

*Fuck. Me.*

I imagine those shoes digging into my back. Then my shoulders. Then the back of my head...

"Hello?" the bunny repeats, her voice like silk. "Ummm... Mr. Richards? Anyone? I've—er—brought the weeklies, and—" As she pivots toward the windows, she cuts herself off with a gasp. It's so quiet up here—seventy stories up from the city—I'm able to hear her whispered follow-up. "Holy *shit*. Is that China?"

"Not quite."

"Oh!"

I bite the inside of my lip to keep from laughing as she nearly leaps like a bunny—only the joke's on me as she wobbles in those precarious heels. I lurch up, jabbing my hands into my front pockets to hide the glowing tips, but see I don't fool her with the "casual" approach. She looks me over, head to toe, her gaze bold and probing and unafraid.

Jesus.

When was the last time somebody stared at me without fear in their eyes?

I don't want to analyze that answer right now. I only want to enjoy the effects of it. The need to move closer to her, even as I feel the danger of her. The fire she ignites deeper in my fingers. The heat she causes to swell to the very tip of my cock. The awareness she opens in all my nerve endings.

Still, I manage to get out, in a tone as suave as how I *used* to sound, "Easy, Velvet. I'm just here for the view too." Only it's sure as hell not the cityscape stretching outside the window.

"My... My name's not Velvet."

"Probably not." I only move my gaze. All the way across the creamy angles of her face. "But it fits." *Velveteen Rabbit.* The book had been one of my favorites growing up. Gerta, my au pair, read it to me so many times. *What does it take to become real...?*

The bunny in front of me now says nothing. She presses the folder tighter to her chest—but I know arousal disguised as decorum when I see it. The recognition draws me closer to her, even though she stiffens and thrusts a stiff hand between us.

"I'm—I'm sorry, Mr. Richards. I'm just going to restart this train and hope I don't wreck it this time." She jogs her chin up, beaming a smile I can only describe as adorable. "Emmalina Crist. It's a true honor to meet you, sir."

Yeah. Adorable. And now, impossible. If I shake that gorgeous hand, she'll wonder why my fingers look like glow sticks and my skin feels like an electric fence. She'll never look at me with such open trust and honor again.

She'll never see me as human again.

So I put on my own masquerade. I give her fingers and their light-pink nails only a casual glance and step back with an air of moneyed asshole before jerking my head toward my darkened office. "You can leave them on the desk, Miss Crist. On your way out."

The edges of her mouth fall, but the optimism doesn't dim from her eyes. "Of course." She sidesteps me—undoubtedly, at last, sensing what everyone usually does. The air molecules that just aren't "right" around me. The freakish "force field" that'll soon have her beelining for the desk and making hurried excuses to leave...

Any second now.

I can only hope.

And dread.

"That desk?" She lifts a tentative finger. "In there?"

I almost laugh. Humor is the heart of pathos, right? I'm sure as hell not going to cry in my milk about giving this woman the creeps from being near me. From what I can tell, she volunteered to play delivery girl on the reports. *Curiosity can kill bunnies too, Miss Crist.* "Unless you want to drop them on the other one?" I murmur. "In the bedroom?"

Her gaze flares. She's not too innocent to miss *that* lob of inappropriate—which baffles the fuck out of me too. I've logged more than my fair share on the bridge of the *USS Man Whore* but have never moored the thing at the company dock. What the hell has made me lose my mind now?

"Does that room have a better view than this one?"

That. Right there. *That's* what made me do it. This woman. This pure, sparkling, open, awe-filled creature, taking my obnoxious overture and turning it into something completely different. Something funny, even sexy. The realization is all my dick needs to surge on board once again, making me clear my throat and turn from her—back to the shadows from which I originally emerged.

"Does that matter?" I'm not sure what I mean by that, only that it'll keep her here a few minutes longer.

"Of course it matters." She follows me in, her steps becoming more confident. "A desk in the bedroom doesn't make sense otherwise."

"Because bedrooms are strictly for romance?"

"Well, they're not for desk-type sh—" She cuts herself off again. "Desk-type *things*." She shakes her head in what can only be a silent self-punishment. "And I'm stepping way out of line again." She lifts a fast wince to where I now stand, between the desk and the all-the-way-to-China view she loves so much. "So I'll just...ummm...drop these here and... Well, good night. *Oh, good night!*"

Her repeat is a full-out shriek as her "casual toss" of the file turns into a different event altogether. Near as I can determine, her shoes are the traitors. She loses balance on one, causing her to overcorrect with the other, but twists that ankle too. She lurches forward, but the file hasn't left her grip. In one impressive burst, every page of the weekly report is now a white flurry in the air, dancing with each other before landing across the desk and at my feet.

"Shit, shit, shit, shit, shit." No self-editing for her this time. She keeps it up, scrambling to grab each page, clearly clinging to the hope of collating them again.

I should tell her to stop. I should reinforce how pointless her cause really is, with fifty-plus pages of data in eight-point font. I should reassure her it'll be easier to recycle this mess and simply reprint the report.

I should. But I don't.

Because fate has given me a bonus gift, and I'm not about to waste it.

Because watching her reminds me of beholding something like the Eiffel Tower or the Taj Mahal for the first time. There'll never be another moment full of all my wonder and none of my breath—

Grabbing me by the center of my balls.

Seizing. Then gripping. Then pounding.

Not even the Eiffel Tower pulled *this* shit.

I clench back a groan. Barely. I reconsider restraint as Miss Emmalina Crist leans across my desk, stretching for a piece of paper on the corner. The woman's ass is a work of art—a canvas I imagine painting with streams of my come as she reaches for her own orgasm instead of some stupid spreadsheet...

"Shit, shit, shit, shit." Yep. She's still at it. "Guess everyone knows who goofed off in charm school, right? How much lamer can one person get?" She pushes back to her feet, only to hurry around to my side of the desk. "Well, the idiot is going to make this right," she blurts. "I promise."

With that, she drops again. To her knees.

*Shit, shit, shit, shit.* Guess it's *my* turn now.

"Miss Crist—"

"Wow. It's all over the place back here."

"Miss Crist—"

"I know, I know. I should've binder-clipped the pages. This won't happen again, I promise. *I promise.*"

"It's all right," I mutter. It's *unreal*, my brain growls back. No. It's completely nuts. This, from the guy who just put three assholes behind bars using electromagnetic bursts and a handful of extension cords. But if the angel fucking Gabriel had descended in here ten minutes ago prophesizing I'd be standing here in the shadows, trying to talk a woman up from her knees while my erection all but throbbed in her face, I'd have laughed him back up to the cloud of crack from which he'd descended.

Last time I checked, the angels knew to leave me alone.

Which means I'm really all alone here. In the dark. With this woman. And her hair and her skin and her curves and her frantic little mutterings, filling the air with an energy I can't comprehend...

Filled with everything except fear.

What the hell?

Why isn't she afraid of me?

Yeah, I'm damn sure she's not.

If I've become an expert about anything since being turned into a walking diode, it's what fear smells, tastes, looks, and feels like. I've experienced it in some form, big or small, from every person on the planet forced to interact with me since those months with "Doctor La Salle" and her gang of torturing freaks. Emmalina Crist is a lot of things right now, but scared isn't one of them.

A realization I refuse to let go.

A treasure I refuse to relinquish.

A woman I refuse to resist.

No matter how wrong it is.

No matter how high Karma sets my payback price.

### E M M A

Weak, weak, weak.

The word pinches my psyche worse than the damn shoes on

my feet. Both are reminders of how I have nobody to blame for this humiliation but myself.

*Weak.*

I had to go and wear the platforms to work, believing the advertising that sold them to me in the first place. I'd be glamorous, sophisticated. I'd at least *look* like I belonged at a job in the big city.

*Weak.*

Glamorous and sophisticated? Look how long they'd lasted from the moment Reece Richards walked in the office door. My massive case of stupidiotic was compounded by this lame excuse to see him alone.

*Weak.*

Stupid *and* idiotic have turned to lunacy up here too, from the instant he emerged from the shadows looking better than the sweeping view. His tie is off. His glasses are on. Why the hell is he the only man on earth who looks better in glasses, not the other way around? The bold black frames are lined in silver, making his eyes seem to glow as he exhales hard and stares down at me.

And stares.

And stares.

Right past the noticeable swell between his legs.

The ridge seems to surge toward me now, beckoning with heat I can feel across my whole face. Swelling as I let out heavy breaths of my own, all too aware of how the air has changed between us. Of how it has charged...

*Oh, my God.*

I want him.

Not just with gee-it's-been-a-long-time lust.

With singular, groundbreaking, life-altering need.

I want him.

More badly than I've ever craved a man before. The desire tears at my muscles, burns at my blood, pounds in every cell of my sex. The papers in my fingers start to rip from my grip—but if I let them go, I know damn well what I'll reach for instead.

"I—" My voice sounds foreign to me. A light year away. Achingly intimate. "I... Maybe I should just—"

"Just what, Velvet?"

*Velvet.* He had to go and say that. Using *that* rasping demand of a tone.

"I should..."

*I should go. You're my boss. I need this job. This is wrong.*

*This is so right, it's terrifying.*

Just for a second, I need to succumb to the rightness. For one mindless moment, I can no longer resist the terror. I let my mind leap over the cliff of my propriety. Fate hasn't brought me to this exact unreal place at this exact unreal time only to be slapped down by a dorky bumpkin from the OC who can't take a massive cosmic hint.

It's just one moment.

Just him and me.

Drawn. Desiring. Surrendering.

The force pulls my head over. I slide through the breath separating my face from his body, brushing my nose across the seam over his crotch. His body jolts. The fabric tautens. He erupts with a harsh hiss while I draw in a deep breath. My senses swirl from his heady scent. His cologne, metallic and smoky. His arousal, musky and thick. Is the fabric under my nose getting damp?

I want to know.

I need to find out.

I press closer.

His tight moan flows down over me, tempting beyond the line we're still just dancing on. Unbelievably, there's still a sliver of room for turning back. We're in silent agreement on that, our muscles tight and our breaths shallow, waiting for the other to leap to their senses and declare this the really bad idea it is...

But it doesn't feel bad.

It feels...

I can't even try to fill in that blank. Nor do I want to.

I just know I don't want it to end. Not yet. *Please, not yet.*

"Miss Crist." Nor does he. His growl, vibrating from a place deep inside him, is my verification.

"Mr. Richards?" I'm not sure if the whisper is a question or a supplication. Maybe both. I revel in how his zipper stretches beneath my lips. He's so big, so hot—and I'm so amazed. I'm on my knees in front of a man but have never felt more powerful in my life. This is beyond anything I've ever thought of doing to anyone. Beyond anything I've ever dreamed.

"Shit."

His hiss is like a rough caress to every inch of my body, every corner of my sex. My hips roll, driven by raw instinct, struggling to alleviate the ache in my core. No. It's not just an ache. It's an instinct, stripped and primitive, twining my every cell to the energy he's heightened since I first felt his eyes on me. It's unbelievable. Unbearable...

And now, unavoidable.

He knows it too. I feel it in the harsh spasms of his muscles. In the growling effort of his breaths. In the energy vibrating so potently between us, I swear the air nearly glows.

Wait. It *is* glowing.

Brighter still, as he stretches his elegant fingers across my periphery, reaching into my hair. Why do each of his nailbeds look like lit fireflies?

"Eyes. Here."

He enforces both syllables by twisting his grip into my hair, the right hand, then the left, compelling my stare straight ahead. I'm consumed with nothing but his crotch once more. The pulsing ridge. The magnetic heat.

"Miss Crist?" It's not a full question, though inflected enough to prompt mine.

"Mr. Richards?"

"Do you want this?"

I wet my lips. "Yes. Oh, yes."

"So swift," he murmurs. "So eager. Yet you don't even know what I want to do to you with it."

I dare a small glance up. His face, encased in lust, will be the centerpiece of my memories for a long time to come. "Will you tell me?" I purposely bite my bottom lip. "If I ask nicely?"

His jaw clenches so tight, a pulse ticks against his stubble. He pulls harder on my scalp. "Nice has nothing to do with what's happening here, Velvet."

Freaking. Hell.

Just like that, he throws open the lid to a new space inside me.

Gives rise to a creature worthy of his electric erotic power. A woman I hardly recognize as me—but wholly, happily embrace.

"Then shut up and just show me."

# CHAPTER THREE

### R E E C E

Could I have prayed for her to say anything better?

Could I have dreaded she say anything worse?

*Show me.*

She has no idea what she's asking for. Fuck. I have no idea what she's asking for, though I can claim the advantage of an educated guess. My four-women-a-month life is a distant memory now, but my dick hasn't forgotten that playboy's needs. Fine-tuning the art of a worthy jerk off has brought some revelations—like the fact that I can now see my jizz, glowing like nuclear waste, as it swirls down the shower drain.

Christ.

How am I standing here, even thinking of exposing this magnificent creature to that danger?

*I'm* not *thinking. At least not about her. Because once again, it's all about me. Guess the saying* is *true. Once an asshole...*

"No." It's a scream in my brain but a grate on my lips as I twist in conflict. The woman at my feet interprets the sound differently. Her raised stare, huge and dreamy and lusty, confirms it. I'm a fucking wreck and she's an aroused rabbit, thinking I'm opting for some coy bid at nobility. I don't know whether to laugh or rage—until both options are ripped away by the woman herself as she reaches to unfasten my pants.

One quick release of my top button and my cock takes full advantage of the extra breathing space. As new blood rushes to my groin, harsh air grunts into my throat. It becomes a full growl as she drags her fingers down the seam of my crotch.

"*Fuck.*"

Velvet rabbit? What the hell was I thinking? She's a seductress, those big blue eyes just the gateway to her temptation, softness and light beckoning me to give up, give in, give over. *It's all right,* she seems to whisper to me. *It's all good. It's so good. It's going to be even better once you're inside me.*

No.

*Yes.*

No.

A gust of wind whumps the windows at my back. A blast of lust fills my cock, turning every motion into torture...and her warm breaths into unbearable teases. With limp surrender, she releases the papers in her grip. They smack to the floor and fan apart, forming a crisp bleached carpet for our dirty, debauched acts.

Corruption I need to end. A goddess I need to let go.

But I can't. *I can't.* Her desire is like a new drug. Her surrender is my new sanity.

I hang on tighter—to bring her face even closer.

She parts her lips and then runs them up and down my hardening ridge. Not a trace of hesitation in her movements. Not a single waver in her low, needy moan. She's a gift. *My* gift...

Which is why I have to make her stop.

Which is why I can't.

"Unzip it," I command in a soft growl.

I won't let her go too far. I'll give her just a taste. I'll stop before she swallows anything. I'll let her lick until the pre-come returns and then I'll pull out and—

"Wow."

Her rasp, so sincere, is joined by her wondering stare as she palms the bulge beneath my briefs. It comes close to being the goddamned sight of the century—close because *that* honor goes to what she gives me in the next second. With a sweet little sigh, she dips in close enough to nuzzle me again. To inhale me...

"Mr. Richards?"

I'm grateful for her soft query. It forces me to focus. To coalesce brain matter into words. "Yes, Miss Crist?"

"You're wet."

Fuck the hell out of me.

Which is so *not* going to happen, even if the effort kills me.

And wouldn't that be Karma's ultimate joke? The player turned freak, throwing himself at petty thieves and thugs in the hopes of taking a stray bullet to his gut, instead put down by his wayward dick. *Step right up, folks. Come and get your poetic justice riiigght heeere.*

But for now, I'm alive. And that means forming words. *Remember those, moron? Get the words out. Keep the come in.*

"And are you?"

She narrows her gaze. Breathes harder. For an incredible second, I can see down her blouse. She's wearing a dark-pink bra under the matching satin blouse. I wonder if the nipples under it are a similar hue. Are they tight from my demand? Have they become erect berries centered in puckered areolas?

"Am...I...?"

"Wet." I all but snarl it out. Maybe if I talk like a monster, she'll begin to believe I am one. "Are you wet too, Miss Crist?"

She shivers. I prepare to watch the fear creep into her gaze, but only clear blue curiosity returns my scrutiny. "I...I think I *am*."

"And that surprises you?"

She furrows her brow. "I suppose it does."

And just like that, my dick fills with new lightning. What the hell? All she's done is touch me through my underwear—but it's enough. Holy fuck, *more* than enough. I'm so goddamned hard, it hurts.

"You should check."

Her gaze widens. "I should...what?"

"Check." I nod curtly, enforcing the mandate. "You heard me. Do it, Emmalina. Pull your skirt to your waist, drop your panties to your knees, and put a finger in your pussy. Then tell me if you're wet."

For the first time, uncertainty clouds her face. Perhaps a little fear. Has she finally grabbed the clue? Realized I'm *not* the lonely Heathcliff up in the tower? That Neeta, Wade, and Fershan are right to be freaked out by me? That *she* should be freaked out by me? But I search her face again and see none of that. I think she's just hesitant about obeying me—about seeking her pleasure in front of me. But I remain implacable. She *will* obey.

"You... You want me to—"

"Touch yourself." I massage her scalp. "Yes."

"While you watch?"

"Every fucking moment."

She twists her lips. "Said the Big Bad Wolf to Red Riding Hood?"

A growling chuckle spills out. "What big eyes I have?"

"What beautiful eyes you have."

My laughter fades. The reverence in her voice... *Fuck.* Now I'm just as awestruck, wildly wondering where the hell this amazing creature has come from—and why the fuck that even matters right now. Not when all I care about is her obedience to my demand.

"You're stalling, bunny." I splay my fingers wider against her scalp. "Do it now. Your finger in your pussy. Watching you will bring so much pleasure to my dick. You're going to make me so fucking hard."

My filthy narrative is the right flip to her switch. She even kicks up a playful smile while bunching her skirt north of her waist, though it vanishes the moment her panties drop the other direction. With one more glance to ensure I'm still serious about my order, she slides one hand south...

Bringing heaven to the seventieth floor.

Heaven, in her guttural gasp of sheer arousal... In the soft drop of her head against my fingers... In the heady musk of her on the air...

Arousal I need her to tell me about.

Heaven I can experience through her.

If just for a moment...

"Tell me." Focusing on the words helps me keep control—at least in the parts where it matters. I focus on their syntax, along with how it aches to push them from my locked teeth, but even that's barely enough. Witnessing her arousal brings on more of my own.

It's fucking near intolerable...

"You... You were right."

Her voice, now husky as whiskey, rolls through me in the same way. She brings torment and salvation together, a pleasure-pain I crave but resist. "About what?" I jerk on her hair, forcing her to stare up at me. "Say it, Emmalina."

She swallows. Dear *fuck,* so gorgeous. "I'm...wet," she stammers. "So damn wet."

"Good girl." At my praise, her skin flushes, her lips fall open, and she drags in heavy air. Dear fuck. *This* is my undoing. The freedom of how she looks at me, offering herself to me... It's like a bolt cutter on some lock inside, a shackle that's been so heavy for so long, I'm not even aware of it anymore. Not until this moment of getting to throw it free, celebrating with a new command for her.

"Now show me."

For a moment, she's confused again. "Show...you...?"

"How wet you are." I dip my head toward her fingers, which still massage between her creamy thighs. In the same instant, inspiration hits. I push down the front of my briefs far enough for my balls and shaft to spring free. If she only gets a taste, I'll make sure it's a damn good one. "Drench your finger with your arousal, and spread it over me—here."

I watch without restraint as she obeys without question. Her touch is full of fascination and adoration as she slicks her juices along my flesh, even taking time to trace over the larger veins, which pulse as if they're going to explode right off my shaft. I'm just as spellbound. Her hair turns into a glowing halo under my fingertips. Her gaze all but worships my cock. And the perfect O of her lips reaches for my tip like a choirgirl about to take communion.

And holy God, do I want to give it to her.

But *she* gives before *I* can. Takes me in, surrounding me with her mouth, displaying the whole fucking universe to my senses in one stroke of heat and warmth and wetness. She sucks me deeper, tightening and expanding that cosmos at once, filling it with the echoes of my mindless moans.

Mindless. That says it all. My thoughts have vanished. Logic, or whatever I thought I possessed of it, is gone. I'm nothing but desire and ache and need, every electron of my body zooming to the crux of my thighs, the length of my cock, the perfection of her mouth.

A groan careens through my head. It's edged in conflict, and for a second I wonder why.

*You can't do this.*

*You could kill her. This could kill her. She's not the one who's supposed to die.*

It's me. I'm the one. And I *am* dying already, my chest locking down air with every new effort at restraint. Before I can control it, a spurt of pre-come erupts out. I force my eyes open, watching her throat convulse on it, praying like hell I haven't scalded her for life...

Her gaze goes wide.

She keens in shock.

*Shit. Damn. Fuck.*

She goes down on my dick like a kid given candy for the first time. Confirms I'm not imagining it by lifting a stare full of brilliant blue arousal before going back to work as if it's fucking Godiva.

"Holy sssshhh..." It's all I'm able to get out before she pulls me in so hard my balls collide with her chin. I'm not hung like an elephant, but my cock is built like the rest of me, length instead of girth, meaning that despite the number of women I've known biblically in my life, getting deep-throated has been a rare and incredible treat.

And never, *never*, as good as this.

No. Forget good.

This is...transformative. An all-access pass to another dimension. My blood converts into light ropes. My consciousness blares. My senses blaze. I fist my hands in her hair until I drive her harder, fucking her deeper, rejoicing in the sweet compliance of her deep, needy moan.

I can't stop.

I can't think.

I can only feed her hunger. Sate my lust. Lunge and push and fuck and need...

And *need*...

Until my balls squeeze tight. My lungs seize on air. My brain turns to toast.

And my universe becomes her.

My life pours into her.

It's the best orgasm I've known. And the worst agony I've ever felt.

*I'm killing her. I'm killing her.*

"Fuck." I finish with a helpless choke, a mix of ecstasy and remorse—who knew I'd ever be putting *those* two in a mental test tube—as the heat keeps sizzling through my cock and spurting into her. She answers every drop with a wanton moan, even grabbing my hips when I try to pull away. She's a creature possessed, and I'm ripped to shreds about stopping her. The last meal of her life is a throat full of my come, and the woman is damn near thanking me for the experience.

I will never leave the depths of hell after I die.

Which may be sooner than I think, because she keeps sucking my dick as if her erotic buffet won't end until she has my blood as well as my seed.

At last, with a harsh hiss, she releases me.

At once, my knees give out.

I plummet next to her, still gripping her head. Damn good thing, because I can force her to look at me. To see the apology, too late to do any good, in my eyes.

"I'm sorry." I kiss her desperately, hating myself more as my dick jerks from the taste of myself on her lips. A snarl rips up my throat as I yank away. "I'm so damn sorry."

Her forehead crumples. "Why?"

I struggle for the right words. *Because you sucked my cock so well, I forgot my own damn name. And, oh yeah, I also forgot about the band of lunatic scientists who turned my blood into electricity a year ago, meaning I just turned you into—*

What?

What the hell *have* I done to her?

I have no answer for that—just as I have no words for what starts to happen to the woman in my arms. Only now do I realize I've harbored some dark fears about what to expect if this ever happened—and the reality before me doesn't match any of them. The lightning fire in her eyes, the ruby tint of her lips, and the sensual flare across her cheeks aren't anything close to the horror of a woman in the last moments of her life.

"Emmalina," I croak in place of kissing her again. "Emma," I revise, daring to stroke her cheek. After the climax, my glowing fingertips have returned to normal. "What can I do? How can I—"

Her high gasp cuts me off. Her body jerks, and she falls against me. I lower to my haunches, letting her sag sideways into my arms. She slides a hand under my shirt, scoring my abdomen in time to her spasms. The second her bare ass lands atop my spent cock, she turns into a ball of sensual slithers. I'm beyond baffled. Is this really what death throes look like?

"What can you *do*?" She laughs, taking me from mystified to disturbed—especially as she grinds her backside harder atop my cock. "Haven't you already done it?"

I rest my forehead against hers. "Fuck. I'm so—"

"Proud of your handiwork?" She ropes both hands around my back and digs her nails into my shoulders. Her eyes dilate, the pupils huge islands in cyan seas. "Well, you should be."

I narrow my own gaze. "I..."

"You want to hear me say it, Mr. Richards? Fine." She gulps hard. "I never thought it could be like this. I never thought *anything* could be like this. Happy now?"

I guess I would be—if I knew what the hell she's talking about.

Like a physical punch, comprehension hits.

As soon as I shove aside my guilt long enough to look at her. *Really* look at her.

The pulse in her neck, throbbing wildly. The needy huffs of her breaths. The subtle swivels of her hips...and the light dew of sweat along their inner curves.

Holy fuck.

My jizz isn't killing her.

It's getting her off. In an insane way. From the inside out.

"Oh, aren't you clever?" She stabs the words at me with a turned-on grin, though the look fades as more arousal jolts her.

I preface my reply with a smirk that feels so fucking good. "Clever?" I drawl. Yeah, I'm dicking with her. Because I can. Because I'm so full of joy right now and can't dance on the ceiling about it. I much prefer watching her pleasure from this prime front row seat. "Miss Crist, I'm not sure I know what you mean."

"The hell you don't," she retorts, laughing, until the invisible arousal stabs her again, arching her hips higher. "Ohhh!" Her nails burrow deeper into my shoulders. I let out a dark snarl, welcoming the pain.

"Tell me," I order. "Don't hold back, Velvet." *Because you just turned my hell into complete heaven.* "I want to hear it all."

She responds with an extended cry, coinciding with her new contortion. "Lower," she finally gasps. "It's... It's flowing lower."

"Toward your pussy?" When she nods, I dictate, "*Tell me, Emma.*"

"Y-Yes. T-Toward my pussy. So hot. So intense. V-Vibrating."

"Yessss." I tuck a hand under the roll of her skirt and press my fingers over her abdomen, picking up on the movement she's describing. Her skin is hot, tingling. Her body is alive, trembling.

"There," she confirms, arching up toward me again. "Now there...and there. Oh, shit. It feels so—"

"*Words*, Emma." I need them. I need to know every damn detail about this. I'm a caveman who's just discovered fire but now needs the instruction book for the blowtorch.

Her head thrashes against my arm. "C-Can't. Just...feeling. So much. So m-m-m-m..."

"Then you'll show me." I run a hand down, pushing against her inner thigh until her most wicked fruit is visible. "Yeah. Just like that."

She breathes harder, the coral and pink layers between her thighs like a rose in a rainstorm, fluttering as lightning strikes their core. I've never witnessed anything more incredible. What guy gets to see every moment of a woman's climax from a viewpoint like this? The clenches of her ass. Her glistening pussy lips clutching around her tight dark slit. The sweet swell of her clit, all but glowing like her hottest ember.

I lean in, gripping one hand into the valley between her torso and thigh, and spread her a little farther. I can see every shimmering drop of the cream she squeezes from her trembling core—now blended with the milk she just drank out of my cock.

"Holy. Fuck."

I rasp it.

She screams it.

I watch, entranced, as she falls apart in my arms—again and again and again.

*And again...*

Every time more of my fluid hits her tunnel and her clit, she's flooded with fresh ecstasy, taking her through wave after wave of wordless pleasure. Every time, I'm taken to a new high by the incredible creature in my arms. How all of this hasn't Tasered her trust and passion is beyond my comprehension, but not my gratitude. She may be the one on her fifteenth climax, but I'm the fucker celebrating the biggest win of the night. I'm holding a gorgeous woman in my arms, watching her lose her shit because of me. I'm mindless, weightless, infinite... A feeling I never dreamed I'd know again. A nirvana I'd written off a long damn time ago.

But now isn't the time for that morose mental path.

Now is about a lightning strike named Emmalina Crist and learning more ways to make her feel good. After what I've just witnessed, I'm not exactly sure how that miracle will be accomplished but am open to exploring the possibilities.

Wait a second. Open? No. *Open* is for trying new food or looking at a new avenue of auxiliary revenue for the hotel. I'm not *open*.

I'm obsessed.

I follow the path of her sated sighs, soon learning she likes circling caresses along the length of her arm. Her groans deepen as I curl my other hand to comb her brilliant blond hair.

After a few minutes filled with nothing but her soft groans, she murmurs, "Mmmm. That feels so good."

I lean over and kiss her forehead. It feels so good, so right. I do it again. Then question myself. *Was* that right? I've never been a post-coital cuddle muffin or whatever the fuck they call it. It's always been easier to live up to the infamy of my media nicknames, all serving as convenient red carpets to roll out before ushering my bedmates right out the door.

But the carpets are still rolled up. The excuses, all gone. No. They've been blasted into obliteration—though not by the force of the lightning in my veins. They've been turned to dust by the woman in my arms. By her artless passion, her captivating honesty... This astounding blend of her and me for which the word *chemistry* feels like a goddamned insult.

She feels right.

Better than right.

She feels fucking *great*.

And no way in hell do I want her anywhere near the door.

Which is why I inhale with determined meaning and answer her with what sounds like sappy pillow talk, but for once I truly mean it. "A lot more where that came from, little bunny."

She snaps open her eyes and a giggle spills off her delectable lips. "Now I *know* I must be dreaming."

I frown. "Why?"

"Because the mighty and mysterious Reece Richards just called me *bunny*—after getting me off so many times, I lost count."

I quirk my lips. "So, I assume it's a good dream?"

She smacks at my chest before sighing again. *That sound.* If Guinevere and Cleopatra sighed like that, no wonder Lancelot and Mark Antony went willingly to their ruin. "Hmmm. If you must know..."

"Yeah." I kiss her forehead. "I must."

"It was *very* good." She curls closer, looking languid and gorgeous. "I just don't want to wake up."

"Then don't."

"Not an option." Her forehead furrows. "I mean, with all due respect, Mr.—ermmm..."

I'd laugh if her uncertainty wasn't so damn palpable. "Why don't you just call me Reece?"

She blinks. Then again. Clearly, she's wondering if this is the point where she wakes up from her dream. Her quixotic smile returns once I dip down and take her lips in a lingering kiss. Damn. She still tastes like passion, mixed with a lot of silken woman. I want to sample her deeper, so I do. Once the soft, slow tangle of our tongues comes to a reluctant end, I realize my face is tight with confusion. I'm nearly thirty years old and only now I am experiencing the best kiss of my life. Some worldly golden boy.

"Hey." Her gentle prompt breaks me out of my funk. "Are you okay?"

I twist a sarcastic smirk. "Isn't that my line?"

Her smirk mimics mine, only she's a lot more adorable. Those champagne-colored pillows mellow into a soft pout as I finger-comb her hair again. The stuff is incredible, strands of gossamer glowing even without the help of my penlight fingers. I could run my touch through them all night.

Her sleepy grumble tells me I might have the chance.

"Reece?"

I grunt in approval. That's so much better than "Mr. Richards."

"Hmmm?"

"You need to stop that."

"Stop what?" It's tinged with a tease.

"That." She scowls, weakly trying to bat my hand away. "I have to get up. I have to...go back."

"Back where?"

"Work." She whimpers, attempting another drowsy protest. "The... The work people. They'll be—"

"Fine." I turn it into a gentle dictate. "They'll be just fine without you for a while, Emmalina."

"But—"

"I said they'll be fine." I embed it into her mind by speaking it into the perfect plane of her forehead. After another brush of a kiss—I can't keep my lips off her and don't even want to try—I stress, "I'll take care of it, Velvet bunny."

Little tremors shake her form, the motions of a giggle without the sound. "Velvet bunny," she whispers, her face drooping against my chest.

I don't say a word until her breaths lengthen and her body slips into the lazy curves of sleep. Only then, as I lift her from the floor and carry her into the bedroom, do I let my mind echo with her whispered word, letting it part the curtains of my memory. A new passage from my treasured childhood book filters to my conscious—and slices into my chest.

*Once you are real, you cannot become unreal again. It lasts for always.*

Always.

It resounds so deep, I rub my chest after sliding Emma beneath the comforter.

Always.

*Fuck.* I'm weaving way too much symbolism into this shit. It's just a stupid childhood memory of a word that never meant much to me—not that it should have, in my world of all-for-me-all-right-now gratification. After Angelique and The Consortium got their hands on me, I compelled it to mean even less. A concept I couldn't and wouldn't accept.

Monsters don't get to have *always*.

And nothing has changed about the monster I really am.

That means this gets to be my always. Moonlit peace. Depths of midnight. A starscape and a cityscape, their silent beams radiating the room. But none of it as beautiful as the person at my side, sleeping through satiation from our passion.

She consumes my attention as I stretch beside her, tracing fingertips along her collarbone and shoulder. She tremors a little and turns toward me.

"Sleep, bunny," I murmur. "I'll watch over you, sweetheart."

For as long as this *always* will let me.

# CHAPTER FOUR

## EMMA

Some dreams are just better than others.

But this one's a freaking Big Mac of better. With extra cheese and secret sauce.

So damn good, a lot of the details climb out of the sleep fog with me. I swear I can still smell Reece Richards on my skin, smoky and spicy. I can feel the lingering warmth of his climax on my throat...and everywhere else.

*Everywhere.*

I roll to my side, twisting the bedcovers against my pussy, moaning into my pillow as the sensitive surfaces swell to life...

As if I really did climax over two dozen times for the man last night.

As he did nothing but watch.

*Impossible.*

But so wonderful to think about.

I trail a hand down and slip my fingers beneath my panties. The world beyond my closed eyelids is still too bright, meaning there's time for at least a quick fantasy before prepping for work. This time,

I'll be awake for it too. *Yessss.*

I roll to my back and kick the covers free, letting the room's warmth drench my skin. I get rid of my panties in an equal hurry, luxuriating in the softness of the sheets and pillows—and do I mean *soft.* New fabric softener for the win. My discount cotton sheets suddenly feel like thousand-thread Egyptian stuff, and I'm damn Nefertiti in the middle of them.

With a fantasy pharaoh filling my mind's eye.

His stare, silver and charged. His face, striking and bold. His body, proud and etched. *Oh, that body.* His chiseled torso pulls my stare in, and I push heavy air through my chest as I trail the gaze of my dream-self down to the best part of him.

Oh.

*That.*

He's magnificent. Undaunted. So unafraid to show me how his cock wants me. I'm not even bashful about using the word *cock.*

My sex clenches as I trail my fingers down, finding the most tender part of my clit. As I stroke those sensitive nerves, my mind blooms with an image of his stalk, long and gleaming and erect...

And delicious.

Oh *yes.* That too.

As if my dream is actually a memory, I relive every moment of pulling him inside my mouth. All the way down my throat. He groans, amazed that I take him so deeply. Even I'm astounded. Somehow, his come has cauterized my gag reflex. I'm able to suck his cock all the way inside. Deeper and deeper...

He grows inside me. Bigger and bigger...

He fucks my mouth. Harder and harder...

I release a sigh. Spread my legs. Dig my heels into the bed, thrusting my pussy into my hand. I moan, rubbing faster. Trying, with urgent need, to keep up with what the dream does to my blood, my nerves, my sanity.

Needy gasps tumble off my lips.

His hungry snarl tangles with them. A beautiful sound...only now it seems so real...

Too real.

I force my eyes open. Every muscle in my body stops. This isn't my little bed nook at my studio apartment. I'm in a room twice that size, in a bed my whole kitchen could fit into, set on a platform overlooking everything between the Brocade and the Pacific Ocean. Golden sun spills over all the buildings, streets, and cars before glimmering on the sea along the far horizon. Just as distant but just as real is a memory of this room by night...from the vantage point of Reece's arms.

*Reece.*

He'd asked me to call him Reece...

I'd agreed...

In the same giddy haze I find myself now...

And never want to leave.

Especially as the man drops his sweats—the only thing he's wearing—and kicks them aside, stepping onto the riser and bumping his knees to the bottom edge of the bed. If I didn't just shudder with ten kinds of new arousal, I'd seriously start wondering about the dream angle again. But *holy shit.*

"This is real." I finish the thought aloud, needing to hear myself speak it. "*You're* real."

"It is." His gaze heats. "I am." He slides one hand around the base of his erection. As he strokes that mesmerizing length, his body tautens into amazing lines of muscle. "And you are. Thank *fuck*."

At once, I start moving too. Any fragment of uncertainty or insecurity is scorched by the spell he casts on me. Is the air sparkling? And if it really is, why am I not surprised? It's him and that bizarre but beautiful force field of his. He ignites my blood and electrifies my pussy in the same incredible second...

Every inch of my intimate triangle cries out, demanding attention. I writhe, shameless in my lust. My thighs start to ache. My nipples pucker, painful and pulsing.

It all gets worse—and better—as he hikes both knees to the bed and scoots his way toward me.

"Spread for me, Velvet."

*Velvet.*

Oh, my God. That wasn't a dream either.

With a surrendering sigh, I obey him. My attention is rapt as he widens his pose, scraping my inner thighs with his knees. The coarse hair covering the amazing muscles of his legs is a deeply primal turn-on. *Take me. Please.*

He keeps fisting his erection. Up and down, up and down, up and down. His strokes are bold and demanding, corresponding to the force of his stare on my body.

"You're so fucking beautiful." The words rasp from between his locked teeth as he leans over, bracing himself with his free hand. "Just looking at you like this... Feel what it does to me."

My gasp twines with his groan as his hand halts on his cock. The muscles in his arm constrict, aiding the extra hard squeeze he gives just under the purple mushroom at his tip. The slit in it brims with a liquid pearl—a drop he aims directly over my clit. We both watch that gleaming bead, hovering...teasing us...

"Oh," I croak. "*Oh.*" When I lift my head, his stare awaits, severe as a dagger and slicing me just as deep. I'm not nearly so sure of myself. Of any of this. Will that liquid, pumped from that wicked place inside him, have the same effect on me as last night? Will it feel as good on the outside of my pussy as it did from the inside? I can barely force my brain around the questions, let alone my lips.

*His* mind and mouth aren't so hesitant.

"You want it, Velvet?"

I shiver from the electric caress of his voice. "Y-Yes."

A corner of his decadent mouth kicks up. "Then you have to say it."

I gulp hard. "I—I want it."

"Say it all. *What* do you want, Emma? And *where* do you want it?"

I groan.

He smirks.

"Please...Reece..."

"*Say it.*"

"I... I want your come. Right here. In... In my pussy."

He squeezes and his liquid drips into my shivering folds.

I shoot to the stars.

The orgasm hits hard and fast. My eyes blaze wide. A scream spirals up my throat and is consumed by Reece's brutal kiss. I give him the sound with open abandon, too shocked and aroused to fight his sweeping, searing attack. His tongue is the center of my world, a life raft of reality in an ocean of unthinking ecstasy. He groans hard in response, the sound emanating from his core as he drips again onto me, making me burst again.

"Ahhhh!" I shriek while breaking away to search for air and logic and what's left of my sanity. "What's going on?" My plea shoots toward the ceiling. "Wh-What the hell are you doing to me?"

The cherubs sculpted into the corners of the crown molding have no response for me. But the man between my legs sure as hell does. He's everything they aren't: full of motion and passion and wicked, wild intentions firing like quicksilver in the depths of his focused stare.

"Doing to you?" he echoes, grabbing my face to angle me for his deep, hard kiss. "Everything I possibly can, Miss Crist. Every*where* I possibly can."

### REECE

"Yes, Mr. Richards."

I'm not sure what turns me on more, the formality she automatically returns to or the submission with which she does. Everything this woman does and says has my cock surging with magma, pressure building, heat increasing, like a volcano about to explode.

There's no more time. Her surrender, open and generous and perfect, is all I've been waiting for.

I slide my hips forward, impelling her legs to widen for me. I aim my aching dick toward her willing entrance, ready to take her pussy with one full push—but stop myself. Fuck. Twelve months of imposed celibacy and I've really gone as stupid as a teenage virgin.

"Damn it." I lower my head and push up a little, breathing hard. Our foreheads are pressed together, so I feel her puzzled frown at once.

"Wh-What's wrong?"

Shockingly, I'm able to grunt out a laugh. "No condoms."

"Wh—" She huffs. Stares at me harder. "Are you kidding?"

"Wish I were." I raise my head a few inches more to study every adorable line of her scowl. "And you don't believe me."

"Would you, if you were me?"

Damn good point. *Probably not.* But hell, I want to change her mind. Right here, right now, I want to give her all the real answers for trusting me. As in, I want to tell her everything. All of it. For just once, for just this woman, I long to come out of the shadows. To trust *her* with everything. The whole truth, from beginning to end, exactly as it happened last year.

Out in the foyer, there's a loud chime.

Emma starts. I break away, springing off the bed.

"What is that?" Anxiety fans her tone. Before I can stab both legs back into my sweats and throw on an old T-shirt, she's clutching the cover to hide her breathtaking nudity.

"Stay here." I curl one knee to the bed, grab the back of her neck, and slam an adamant kiss to her lips. "We're not done yet."

Not by far.

I shut the bedroom door and clear the hallway into the foyer just in time to plaster a professional smile on my lips. It's enough of a reply, at least for the moment, to the questioning gaze in the pretty face of the woman stepping off the elevator.

"Miss Jain. Good day. What can I do for you?"

## EMMA

"Shit, shit, shit, shit."

I rasp it at least twenty more times while peeking through the crack in the door at Reece and Neeta. I've dragged the comforter off the bed with me, certain Reece has simply gone to sign for a package or something. But now I'm gaping at my boss, who stands there with *her* boss, less than ten feet from where I flailed and screamed like a porn star last night. While *he* watched.

Yeah. I've finally realized it wasn't a dream.

And no, I'm not thrilled about that fact.

Especially because I can't see if Reece had the time or inclination to clean up after our debauchery last night.

And holy wow, what debauchery.

I let my head drop into my hands and succumb to a nearly silent sob. This is fate's version of ultimate sarcasm, but it's not funny. I've finally escaped the OC, gained freedom, independence, and a great job, only to risk it all because I got horizontal with my tantalizing god of a boss—who, by the way, also happens to be the most amazing lover on the planet.

And no, I don't need to sample the rest to be sure of that.

My attention rivets back to the discussion in the foyer. Neeta's talking about me—and looking pretty stressed about it.

*What the hell?*

"...can't believe she fell ill like that so fast." Her hair catches the sunlight coming through the same bank of windows that caused my holy-shit-is-that-China gawks a few hours ago. She's dressed in the same suit she wore for last night's shift, making me realize it isn't as late in the day as I first thought, though she still looks as fresh as the moment we first clocked in. I'm not sure if I admire her or hate her for that, especially as she executes a classic toss-toss of her ebony mane. The move would've likely preceded a sweet and worshipping smile at Reece if the subject matter weren't my health. I can't even blame her. Reece is, as Wade and Fershan would phrase it, "clickbait for the chicks' sake." I'm not sure of that definition, but it's close enough to "freaking hot" that Neeta's thin ruse of a flirt is no-brainer obvious.

"Stomach bugs can be capricious," Reece responds diplomatically. "Which was why I insisted on calling a car for her. She wasn't in any condition to drive."

Neeta's head jogs to the side. "She told you that?"

I'm oddly tempted to restart the shit-shit-shit litany as Reece takes a second to consider her question. I'd have thought a man who spent more time on nightclub couches than conference calls would be better at bluffing, not worse.

"Not in so many words," he finally says, re-earning his master bullshitter stripes. "She wasn't really in the mood to...talk."

Neeta's forehead pinches. "Oh. I see." Though I wonder if she really does—another instinct I'm unable to verify, since she clearly forgets the thought behind it once Reece folds his arms, returning to pharaoh mode. The move—so arrogant it can only be pulled off by a man of his glory—stretches his clothes across his muscled limbs until Neeta defaults into flustered-and-faltering mode. I don't blame her. I'd be doing the same—if I weren't so preoccupied with wanting to brain the man.

"Well, then." She readjusts the shiny red purse on her shoulder.

"May I be forward and ask if she followed up with you...to let you know she got home all right? I normally worry because she insists on taking the train home, but if you had a driver take her—"

"He called after the drop-off. Told me she got in fine."

I swallow hard. The easy undertones in Reece's voice are gone. He's lying through his teeth and not happy about it.

It's so time for *shit-shit-shit*ting again.

Instead, I let the comforter drop and dart into the bathroom, hoping beyond hope he somehow brought my—

*Yes.*

My suit has been placed onto a couple of hangers that dangle from the side of a door to the connecting bathroom. As I shimmy into my skirt, I fling a longing gaze to the palatial setup of the space. Roman tub with jets. A shower so big it has a seat. A little vanity area with a mirror lined in adjustable lights. In a little side room, there's a toilet with an electronic bidet extension.

I'm thiiiiis close to letting the skirt fall in the name of honoring this bathroom by having sex in it, but then Reece's voice bleeds through the door beyond the bed. He's still uncomfortable about the charade for Neeta's sake—a pretense *he* propagated, I might add—but I'm not about to sit around and extend the fib any longer.

With a few twists, I reattach enough of the buttons on my blouse to get out of here without flashing the world. The effect is better once I get my suit jacket on, especially because there's no time for the whole bra thing. It, as well as my panties, can be his souvenirs for the blue-ribbon debauchery.

Hell.

*Debauchery.*

No way will I ever be able to hear that word again and avoid remembering last night's precious, perfect, mind-altering version of it...

Or the man who gave all that wickedness to me.

The man I now have to escape at all costs. No matter what.

I need this job.

I. Need. This. Job.

Not just keeping it. Thriving in it. Excelling at it. Showing Mother and Lydia and everyone else at the club that "little Emma" *is* capable of succeeding in the big, evil city. That *their* checklist for happily ever after doesn't have to be mine. That not everyone on the face of the earth measures success with a house that sleeps thirty, a car that transports ten, and a passport that's stamped in Paris, Milan, and London.

My checklist is bigger.

So much bigger.

It starts with this job. And does *not* include shacking up in the penthouse with my boss.

I need to get out of here. Now. Before he finishes chitchatting with Neeta. The second her elevator returns, he'll be back in here, frying my resolve with his force field magic.

I creep to the door on the other side of the room, praying it leads to a back corridor of some sort. The front elevator that brought Neeta up isn't the only way into this place. Reece himself usually gets up here via the private elevator in back, which is located somewhere along this side of the tower.

I crack the door and sneak down a short hallway until I enter the kitchen. Still a good sign. The back elevator is also the service elevator for the suite, so direct kitchen access makes sense.

I step across a polished black wood floor and through a culinary spaceship made of glass and stainless steel. Side-by-side ovens, a fully stocked wine cooler, and a coffee bar nearly induce me to another orgasm—okay, so maybe I do miss a few creature comforts from the golden land—but there's no time for more than a few drops of drool right now. I need to locate that back elevator.

*Ding ding ding.*

A small anteroom also turns out to be the landing for the elevator. I pad across it and stab the call button for the car. "Please, please, please," I whisper, hoping the car is already parked at this level, but since Reece came up in the main elevator last night, I have to wait while the system brings it up.

Thankfully, the gears work fast. Not so thankfully, as I hurry into the car and jab the button for the ground floor, the last sound I hear from the penthouse is Reece's unmistakable baritone, bellowing my name from the bedroom. His voice all but topples the walls between us, thundering straight to my belly, making me wrap both arms around myself.

As the doors shut, I lean against the elevator's back wall, seeking solace from the silence that encompasses me.

I'm doing the right thing.

I'm doing the right thing.

I'm doing the right thing.

And soon—*please God, soon*—the rest of my senses will catch up to the strength of that mantra.

Because right now, it feels freaking useless.

# REECE

Useless. This all feels fucking useless.

Even as I pulse yet another asshole bank robber into the waiting arms of the cops, I can't escape the ruthless claw of my feelings. Eight thwarted crimes in three days, and goddamnit, there's still nothing in my gut but half a bean-and-cheese burrito and a shit-ton of unanswered rage.

Fury that seems to have only gotten worse since the moment I stood in the penthouse kitchen, watching the numbers over my private elevator doors descend—and never come back up again.

Ramping up the Dudley Do-Right gigs have only made the rage worse. It's like a field of electric towers in my brain right now, buzzing louder and louder, pushing the limits of my skull thanks to the screams of the civilians, the wail of the sirens, and the antics of the scumbag himself.

"Yeah!" As the officers scoop him off the floor, he jumps a few feet, a victorious grin on his face. "I was zapped by Bolt, y'all! I was zapped by Bolt!"

"Fuck," I mutter while whipping a double take at the asshole, who's juiced more by the cheering crowd. "What the hell?" I bellow, unsure whether I mean it more for him or them. Why can't everyone calm the hell down and get back to work and their lives? On the other hand, why the fuck do I care?

My confusion triggers his. "What the hell, what?" He nods, indicating my leathers—necessary attire despite the fact that it's nearly ninety outside today. "Come on, man. You're really him, right?"

"Him *who*?"

"You serious?" Harsh snort. "You really don't know?"

A chuff comes from the cop double-checking his cuffs. "He's probably been too busy lately to notice the news, asshole. You know, dealing with scumsuckers like you?" He tips a grin my direction. "Some of us are just more grateful than others for it."

I return his compliment with a glare. The move dances on the edge of asshole in its own right, but my bafflement doesn't know the difference. "The news about what?"

"You have a name now, buddy," the cop supplies.

A headache develops behind my scowl. "A *what*?"

"A name." He chuckles. "What? You don't like Bolt?"

"Bolt?" I pronounce the word so slowly, it almost becomes two syllables.

As two more officers come in and haul the criminal out, he's given the physical freedom for a shrug. "Beats 'super hero dude in tight leather,' yeah? Unless you're all about the look?"

"Sure." Now I soak it in sarcasm.

"That's what I thought too." He takes a step closer, going for a just-between-us-guys kind of thing, though giving his true outlook away by glancing over at his buddies with a shit-eating smirk. *Look at me. I'm chattin' it up with Bolt.*

Bolt.

Shit.

As nicknames go, it's not the worst. If I were a dog, I'd be something like a Doberman or a Great Dane, right? Considering how I've chosen the mongrel therapy route this week, I should have seen this coming. *Dog discovers toy. Dog really likes toy. Dog loses toy.*

*Dog deals by pissing electricity all over the city.*

Or something like that.

"Figured with all the power you're throwing around, the suit helps keep it in check. Something like that?"

"Yeah."

Speaking of moving on...

Though the cops still have the bank lobby locked down, the blare of camera lights through the tinted windows alerts me I've overstayed my welcome at this party. The cop, Officer A. Feliz according to his name badge, could've been a guy I'd hang with for a while, pounding beers and playing darts. The old Reece likely would've suggested such a thing. Hell, the new Reece likes the idea too. But the two Reeces don't get to share a universe. It was part of the deal I made with Karma. The bed I made and now must lie in.

Where I'm having issues with Karma is the bridge between figurative beds and real ones.

Like the one in which I'd finally felt alive for the first time in a year. Alive because of the goddess who'd slept in my arms. White-gold hair, cream silk skin, sated sighs. Who'd stayed the night. The whole night.

The first woman—the first *person*—who'd given me a gift more important than all the shiny objects I've possessed in my twenty-nine years of existence.

Hope.

I'd fought it that night. Damn, how I'd fought it. But after those hours of holding and smelling and breathing her, the sensation took root. The sliver of belief, however tiny, that maybe Karma would be merciful and give me one person who didn't feel like crawling out of their skin just because I was in the room. That maybe, just maybe, I didn't have to think about every day of my life going down just like this one.

Waking up alone.

Putting some bad guys away. Saving a few thousand people.

Going to sleep alone.

For a few amazing hours, I'd let myself think otherwise. Held the gift in my arms. Savored it. Treasured it. Been able to shove aside the fact that this nickname they've given is more ideal than anyone realizes.

Bolt.

Why the hell not? It's the way I've treated my own life for so long. Why shouldn't it be the way I'm treated now?

Why shouldn't it be the word I'm celebrated with as I crouch low, surrounded by cheers I barely hear, and sprint from everyone's view—and in a few minutes, from their minds too—as their lives go on again, secure because of the super hero they can forget as swiftly as a tabloid magazine cover?

Again.

MISADVENTURES WITH A SUPER HERO

# CHAPTER FIVE

### EMMA

"Seriously?"

I can barely huff it out before I'm approached by a swarthy ponytailed guy standing next to a spotless stretch Mercedes parked in front of my apartment building. He flashes me a crooked grin. "Well, good afternoon to you too."

I jab up my chin. "We agreed on this, Z. Yesterday was going to be *it* for this nonsense."

He adds a shrug. "It's not an imposition. I wasn't doing anything else."

"You're so full of shit."

The smile takes on a cute quirk. "Fine. You're right. Go ahead and gloat. You want to."

I resist the pull of his Armenian charm. "I swear by the planet you're named after *and* the insane god who created it—"

"Don't care about *that* god," Zalkon volleys. Yeah, a planet. Poor Z came along after his mom binged on *Star Trek* during mandatory pregnancy bedrest. "But the god who's making sure you get to and from work in this every day?" He jerks a thumb toward the Mercedes.

"*Him*, I care about."

I'm tempted to yank out my phone and call said god-on-high. I have a direct line to his cloud. The all-powerful, all-knowing, overprotective Zeus in the penthouse has made damn sure I have the digits all but tattooed on my brain, thanks to his hourly texts for the last three days. Creepy? Under normal circumstances, yes— but what's been normal about Reece Richards's arrival in my life? Everything about this, about *him*, is a flash storm from fate, sizzling through my atmosphere and frying all my circuits. Yeah, including the man's texts.

Even the one vibrating the device in my palm right now—then quivering all the way up my arm, over my shoulder, and down my spine, gripping my whole torso in tendrils of heat I can no more ignore than my own breaths.

"Sorry," I mutter, turning from Z. "Just let me get this."

"Uh-huh."

I ignore his knowing jibe while swiping at the phone with the zeal of an Austen heroine opening a secret love note. I was responsible as hell getting myself out of the man's bed—*not* a decision my hormones let me forget during the solitary ride in the penthouse's private elevator—so I'm due the indulgence of at least knowing I'm still in the man's head. It's not like the situation's going to last. Nothing in the world of Reece Richards does, including models and actresses who spend the equivalent of my monthly salary on a single facial. Last year, the press didn't know what to do with themselves when he spent—gasp—a whole six months with some power blonde from France, and I'm nowhere near her league. I have to be real about that. I'm just a diversion during the man's quest for his next piece of sparkling arm candy.

But I refuse to feel badly about at least enjoying the ride.

*The guy in the tower is thinking of you from the velvet clouds.*

Oh, yeah. He *is* good.

Too good.

I tilt my head, pondering the swoony wordage. This poetic shit is his version of outright chatty—and therefore, a huge tell. What's he hiding? And why does my radar instantly ping it in tones of melancholy?

"Get over yourself." I mutter the mandate at myself while tapping out a reply.

*Good afternoon to you too.*

The marine layer is thick over the city today, never achieving its normal noontime burn-off. That means, seventy stories up, he's texting from another world.

*How does the muck look from the spire?*

I think of adding a winking emoji but refrain. He'll get the humor without the emoji, though the reference didn't start with us as a laughing matter at all. Our first text exchange after *the night*—my private reference to all the so-good-but-so-wrong that went down in the penthouse—was definitely not Austen-novel material.

*EMMALINA.*

*I'm right here. No need to shout.*

*You're NOT right here. Where the FUCK are you?*

*I had to go. You know that too, even if you don't want to admit it right now.*

*I ordered you to stay in that bed.*

*But I never belonged there to begin with.*

*WHAT THE HELL?*

*Stop shouting.*

*We are not done.*

*It was great, Reece. It was beyond great. But you're you and I'm me.*

*And that means what?*

*You live in a spire.*

*Irrelevant.*

*You have a private elevator.*

*Irrelevant.*

*You sign my paychecks!*

*Paychecks you risk your life to earn!*

*Excuse me?*

*You're not taking the train to or from work again, Emma.*

*EXCUSE ME?*

*Who's shouting now?*

*You don't get to be the boss outside that spire, Mr. Richards.*

*We'll see about that, Miss Crist.*

And here I am, about to let him prove his point again. Zalkon—who's propped against the car's back bumper and waiting for me to climb in—will catch hell if I don't. Not to the tune of being strung up by his toenails or anything, but if I pull a disappearing act, Reece will undoubtedly let Z go. And he'd only be replaced by a new driver tomorrow—and by one who wouldn't be half as cool. Besides that, Z's banking the extra money from this gig with Reece to surprise his daughter with a birthday trip to Disneyland.

I nod to Z so he'll open the car door and do my best to snort instead of smirk as the god in the clouds finishes his reply to my query.

*The muck isn't muck at all. Not from up here.*

I breathe a little easier. No more melancholy vibes, which were probably all in my imagination to begin with.

Unbelievably, my own mother's words echo in my head. *Oh, Emma. You and that oversensitive imagination.*

During my musing, Reece has had time to type a new note.

*As a matter of fact, it looks like a giant pillow-top bed.*

His words make me squirm. Not noticeably. Just enough to remind my brain what happens to my body when it joins the idea of Reece Richards to the concept of a bed. Especially one made of clouds.

*Only thing missing is a beautiful bunny with eyes like this sky.*

I quit the squirming to make time for a sigh. This man and the way he can get to a point—most critically, the sensitive one between my legs.

But then there's the other point. The one I can't help returning to, over and over.

*I'm sure you can call other pets to hop across that bed.*

The three dots from his end instantly start dancing. My heart lurches to my throat, though I keep it from climbing all the way up the pipe by climbing into the car.

*I'm strictly a rabbit kind of guy these days.*

Well, that takes care of that. I can feel my heartbeat all the way to my tongue now—the tongue that sneaks out, nervously wetting my lips, as I struggle to turn him down with words that are coy but real, witty but firm. Damn it, where's my inner Emma when I need her? Not the *me* Emma. The other one. The one Mother named me after. The one played by Gwyneth Paltrow, full of willowy charm and outfitted in flowy dresses.

*I have to go to work now.*

She's not in that damn text, that's for sure. Nowhere even near it.

But maybe that's a good thing.

Maybe I need to honor the other Emma a little bit more. The Emma who artfully presents a well-turned ankle to land a viscount to be the center of her worship. The Emma who wants so much more than the viscount, even if he *can* offer clouds like pillows—and a work commute with air-conditioning and leather seats.

*I can't wait for you to get here, either.*

And sends texts like that.

Which I can't help but tease him about. Just a little.

*So I can start contributing to the Richards dynasty again?*

*So you can contribute to my sanity again. When I know you're safe.*

Okay. Texts like *that* too.

Which, damn it, tangle my thoughts like the traffic Z guides the Mercedes through to get onto the 110 toward downtown.

Is it possible the other night *wasn't* just a quick fuck for him? Can it be Reece Richards felt the same electric connection I did? Is it even conceivable to think I'm not a temporary trinket for him? But if so, is that even what I want? I moved here to prove I could do this by myself. To prove I could face scary new stuff and be all right.

Ironic plot twist of the year.

"Scary new stuff" has never had a better definition than what I experienced with Reece Richards three nights ago. Than all the things he still makes me feel every damn day, even from way up in that spire.

Which circles me back to the same unnerving question.

Do I *really* want to know if he feels the same way?

There's only one answer to that.

I don't.

Because as fearless as the new Emma is, the old one is still afraid his answer will be no.

And even more afraid it'll be yes.

### REECE

I stop typing, my fingers suspended over the keyboard.

I let a smile grab the corners of my lips.

*She's here.*

The bizarreness of this isn't lost on me—but no way am I fighting it. In a building filled with hundreds of others, I can feel her. The charge in every ion. The shift in every current. The awakening through the whole building. Through every inch of me. Every drop of my blood. Every electron in my nerves. Every pore of my skin.

Every inch of my cock.

*Damn.* Nobody else has done this to me before. Only her. Only Emmalina. She's pushed me to the edge, and I can't wait to go all the way over. For the last three days, she's made it possible to wake up with a smile on my face again—and even to skip the ritual of the daily prayer I utter over morning coffee. The one in which I beg for the day to finally bring my death.

Yeah, that one.

I need to see her again. I'm tired of avoiding the admission, like some soaked cat sidestepping a rain puddle. Of letting *her* sit on the other side of the puddle, equally afraid.

*Afraid.*

I'm so damn tired of that word being a part of my daily vocabulary.

*Fuck the fear.*

It's the mantra in my head as I step off the Brocade's elevator at the second floor and make my way to the staff conference room. Those words repeat themselves in time to the steps I take down the hall, confirming the rightness of this move—an action I haven't taken in a long damn time for a woman.

Walking into the middle of her turf.

Of course, she doesn't know that yet—nobody down in the management conference room does—which, I realize at once, is kind of a cool thing. Even a full minute after I step into the room, I remain silent in the doorway, studying their tight huddle over what looks like a long rooming list.

Invisibility. It's kind of nice.

For now.

I study the bunch of them, pumped and energized, crediting the extra electricity in the air to their own power. But the best part? I get to gaze at Emma in the same unguarded state. She faces away from me, leaning with one hand on the table, her hair a white-gold cloud thanks to some claw-clip thing. But enough of those entrancing tendrils fall loose that I conjure a fantasy of yanking them free, one by one, as I slide into her again and again, screwing her with carnal intensity...

As if the force of my vision is fierce enough to heat her thoughts—and who says it isn't—her head suddenly lifts. I'm mesmerized by how the motion elongates her neck, exposing an adorable mole in the middle of her nape, before she whips her head around.

At once, the world falls away.

And I'm lost in the endless blue skies of her eyes.

Two seconds of heaven before reality pushes back in. Fucking bastard.

The rest of the management team—I don't even know some of their names, and for the first time in my life, that's *not* cool—go restless and jittery, exchanging self-conscious glances. I stick to my act of glib and impervious, knowing I'm a double whammy of discomfort for them. The brooding boss man who never comes down from the tower and the freak who brings his special brand of weird to the air.

"Mr. Richards!" Neeta Jain pushes through the small throng, putting physical form to their nervousness with her rapid steps. "What a pleasant—"

I stop her with an upraised hand. "Pleasant isn't the first word springing to anyone's mind right now, Miss Jain." I sweep a knowing look around the room. "But maybe I can change that, at least a little."

"Pardon me?"

I arch a questioning brow. "This *is* the rescheduled time for the weekly management meeting? My calendar was pinged about the change."

The woman eyes the phone I hold up. "*Oh*. Of course you were. Yes, of course. Because you're the general manager."

"Of course." My jibe isn't lost on everyone. Chuckles ripple through the crowd behind her, but Neeta's smile is just as forced as before. "*Relax*," I finally admonish the woman. "I'm just going to sit all the way over here and listen in, if that's okay."

The majority of the faces shift from expressions of amusement to happy surprise. The only abstaining votes on the referendum come from Neeta and Emma. While Neeta is still cautiously confused, my gorgeous velvet girl looks more like she's wrapped in sandpaper. Out of everyone in the room, she expected my appearance the least—and sees through it the fastest. Both recognitions only deepen my smirk. I like being the one to catch her off guard, but I also like being the one she can see right through—to an extent. No one on earth will ever know everything about me. Just the way I like it.

"Goodness." Neeta's murmur is full of warmth. "The gesture is certainly appreciated, Mr. Richards. And under normal circumstances, it *would* be okay..."

"But today isn't normal?" I ask.

"Define 'normal.'"

The crack is made in tandem by Wade and Fershan. Though Neeta flashes them a you-did-*not*-just-say-that-in-front-of-the-owner's-son glare, she goes on, prefacing with a light laugh. "*Ab*normal is what we do around here, Mr. Richards. Tonight, thanks to our incredible friend Bolt, we all just have to do it a little faster."

"More than a little." Emma flicks a dismissive glance my way before jogging her head back toward the rooming list, now joined by a housekeeping shift sheet and guest room floorplans.

Unbelievably, I roll with her little snub. Perhaps am even grateful for it. She'll fracture my attention, and right now I've got to focus on Neeta's fresh news and then alter my convenient excuse for coming down here. Thank fuck I've logged some experience with the suave-under-stress thing. Granted, that practice has mostly come from listening to supermodels whisper their plans for my cock while standing in the middle of red carpets, not nodding as an employee refers to my alter ego as her "incredible friend."

*Grit your teeth. Calm your eyes. Pretend you care about what everyone else is talking about.*

At least that last one's not a stretch.

"Bolt." I poke the tone into the realm of a question and tilt my head with equal curiosity. "Are you referring to a person or a laundry detergent?"

Everyone in the room laughs—and they're sincere. It's a bigger gift than any of them realize, incentivizing me to toss a smile down the length of the table. It slams into new waves of disquiet. I can feel everyone's apprehension, as if a switch has been flipped at the same time. Can I blame them, after the invisible amps I've tossed first?

"Bolt is a person." The second Neeta addresses my question, her face crunches. "At least I think so."

"Dude's definitely not laundry soap," Wade utters.

A petite redhead next him bites her lower lip. "*Definitely* not."

"He's a badass," someone else declares.

"A god." The redhead sighs.

"Won't argue there," Neeta murmurs.

"The man is looking for a serious answer." Fershan stabs them with a glower.

"I *was* serious." The redhead throws back as much attitude.

Neeta quells them with a calming hand. Turns back to me. "They're calling him a super hero."

There are times for suave, and then there are times suave can screw itself—or whatever the hell it wants to do as I surge forward. "Excuse the hell out of me?"

"More accurate," Fershan puts in.

"And so much more *serious* than 'god,'" the redhead retorts.

"And none of it matters right now." Emma whirls, stabbing a frown at them both, instantly resetting me to suave mode. My composure is still a masquerade but the only logical choice. No way can I let my whole staff witness how fast this woman gives me wood when flaunting her finest case of peeved. God*damn*, she's resplendent. How the hell have I stayed away from her for three days?

Inwardly, I put Karma on notice. Tonight, no matter what it takes, this heart-halting dream of a female will be mine again.

With my gaze still glued on her, I nod slowly. "Yeah. I remember something about him on the news a few days ago. Looks like a motocross poser? Disappears once the cops get on scene?"

"Doesn't disappear." Wade steps forward to assert it. "Just bolts so fast, it looks like he does. Get it?"

Though I render agreement with a jerk of a brow, the redhead—her name badge appropriately reading *Scarlett Firenze*—now decides to buddy up with Fershan for a shouted, "*Gotta bolt*! Whoop!"

Holy fuck.

Emma gives up her frown long enough to join the group in a cheer. Holy fuck, the sequel. Silver lining? The residual humor on her face turns into stunning glints in her eyes, blazing as she turns and explains, "Obvious morale boosts aside, Bolt's benefiting the city in more ways than he ever intended. Especially downtown, where he's been focusing his adventures lately."

I'm tempted to laugh. Instead, I arch a brow. "Adventures?"

Her giggle is like bright bells. "Ass-kickings? Escapades? Bold acts of mind-boggling bravery?"

"You could really keep that up, couldn't you?"

"Yeah." Another little laugh, infusing the air with more warmth. "Probably." Then even more laughing, shooting white-hot flares through my nervous system. "But I won't." She nods again at the rooming list. "Because of him, occupancy for tonight just went from thirty-five percent to ninety-eight percent. We're hoping to call a full house by midnight."

"Holy fuck." I utter it aloud now, indulging a laugh of my own. Talk about things I couldn't have predicted.

Wade strides over. "Dude's been on fast-forward the last few days. Everything from putting down bank robbers to yanking kittens out of trees from here to Ojai and back. The national news feeds have started carrying updates, and now the guy even has global followers."

I deepen my scowl. "Followers? What do you mean?"

Fershan holds up his phone. Sure enough, there I am. Out of focus, yes. Masked, yes. But the header on whatever social media platform it is—they all look eerily the same lately—proclaims me as *Your friend Bolt: Making vibrators obsolete.* My gaze bugs wider at the number of followers. "Holy shit."

"You mean holy *ker-ching*." Wade smirks. "Because a whole bunch of those"—he stabs a finger at Fershan's phone—"are about to be a whole lot of those." He sweeps the same finger upward, indicating the nearly empty guest room tower over our heads.

"A tour group." As Neeta explains the point further, she pulls off her blazer. Only now do I realize her normal shiny business blouse isn't beneath it. Instead, she's wearing a polo shirt with the Richards Resorts logo embroidered in the upper right corner. "They left Santa Barbara this afternoon bound for Anaheim but chose downtown LA instead."

"Yeah, baby." Wade pumps a fist. "A Bolt in leather is now hotter than the world's most famous mouse."

"*Anyhow*." Emma stresses the point by peeling the light sweater away from her own shoulders, revealing a shirt that matches Neeta's. "With the last-minute booking, housekeeping didn't know to staff up for a fast turn, so the management meeting has been replaced by room-flip duty."

She beams a gloating grin while delivering the news. I say nothing, letting her have a moment of thinking she's done with dealing with me for the night. But only a moment. When it's over, I shuck my jacket and roll up my shirtsleeves. "Excellent. What floor do you need me on?"

As I expected, she thuds into silence. As I also foresaw, she's not the only one—though I can't blame the group for going slack-jawed. I throw my shoulders back, returning the questioning stares with one of conviction. This is different, shaking people up for good reasons—and not when they're about to piss their pants because I just yanked a robber out of their face or levitated their cat out of a tree. This feels pretty good. Actually, this feels *damn* good.

"Mr. Richards." Neeta spreads her arms. "That's so kind of you, but—"

"But what? You're shorthanded, right? Then let me help."

Everyone but Emma—who still pierces me with those twin irises of electric blue—exchanges skittish glances. With arms still open, Neeta approaches me like a trainer would a wild lion. "We were going to tackle the rooms in teams of two."

"And there're thirteen of you here." I lift my winning grin. In my other life, I called it *the look*, a deal-closer that scored me everything from sold-out concert tickets to top-shelf booze. Right now, it only turns the woman's patient smile into a forced grimace.

"Really, Mr. Richards. It's not necessary."

"Oh, for the love of"—Emma wheels around—"*I'll* partner with him." She mutters it like the kid taking her turn with the tag-along little brother.

"How big of you." I add a slight bow to my drawl.

"Emma." Neeta's tone is terse, her lips barely moving. "You don't have to—"

"She'll partner with me."

My growl isn't answered by anyone else. There's no more time anyway. The team gets down to business, quickly dividing up assignments for the rooms. The entire time that's happening, Emma stabs fresh glares my way. I return them with the Zen stare of a jujitsu master, having more fun than when I leveled everyone in the room with my surprise appearance.

And it's not the first time I plan on getting my way tonight.

# CHAPTER SIX

**E M M A**

Damn it.

On about twenty different levels.

How many times have I resolved not to end up in exactly this situation, with exactly this man, over the last three days?

Okay, not the *exact* same. In the scenarios I've been banishing from my imagination more adamantly than chocolate mint ice cream during PMS, I haven't had a dusting mitt on one hand and a porta-vac in the other. A rhino-sized housekeeping cart hasn't been wedged between us in the back elevator.

And Reece hasn't looked half this good.

Cheese and rice, there has to be a law against the man getting even hotter when covered in dust, dander, and sweat from changing bed sheets, scrubbing showers, and replacing coffee packets. With his sleeves rolled up, dark stubble shadowing his jaw, and chunks of his thick hair tumbling over his glasses, he's like a dirtied-up version of a Rolex ad.

Oooooh. *There's* an idea.

On the other hand, I'm fairly sure I'm the first person on the planet who's ever seen him like this, and I'm not certain I want to share the privilege with everyone else. It feels...special. Intimate. Inaugural. Several times over the last hour, I've caught the man peeking in mirrors and windows, as if even he doesn't recognize himself. When *was* the last time he busted his ass for someone other than himself? Though technically, the effort *is* still about him. In one way or another, some of tonight's windfall for the Brocade will breeze back over to him—but it's still nice to see him actually acknowledge that fact.

"Sewing kit for your thoughts."

I leave my musings with a giggle, accepting his offer of the room amenity. Both his arms are folded over the top of the housekeeping cart, accentuating the breadth of his shoulders and the muscles in his forearms. Dear God, how I want to lean forward and explore those striations...with my tongue...

*Which would make you different from Lydia and all her tennis club gal pals...how? Which would prove your resolve that life can be about more than a man, a mansion, and the most perfect lawn on the block...how?*

"Do I need to offer a pillow chocolate for your thoughts too?"

I smirk and reach for the little foil circle just as the elevator dings and the doors open at our new floor. "And *that's* what I've been holding out for."

But at the speed of light, he snatches my chocolate prize out of reach and the entire cart off the elevator. For a second, I stand and gawk, wondering what trick I've just missed—though the Muzak version of Ed Sheeran's latest hasn't progressed more than a handful of notes.

"How...the hell..." I struggle for words that won't make me sound six kinds of crazy. Not that he's listening. I race to keep up with his long strides down the hall, concentrating on matching two of my steps for every one of his.

"Hop to it, little bunny." He moves with lithe grace even while towing the massive cart, making my throat go dry. It's one thing to flip through gossip magazine pictures of his globe-trotting exploits but another thing to witness the natural athleticism required for adventures like cycling the Dolomites, kayaking in Costa Rica, snorkeling in Tulum—and those are only the locales I can recall. "We're on a schedule," he says while waving a keycard to unlock our next room.

Room being an understatement.

We're now tackling our first suite on the rotation, and it's one of the biggest in the hotel. The view is nearly as incredible as the one from the penthouse—not a surprise, since we're just two floors lower. I gasp after pulling the drapes open and stop for a moment to simply stare. The city is a twinkling carpet tonight, cars forming moving threads in a tapestry of mostly amber, emerald, and cobalt. In the distance, the towers of Century City stand like diamond-studded obelisks.

"Wow." I can't help but murmur it, though I congratulate myself on refraining from China references this time.

"You mean that, don't you?"

I gasp again—this time from wondering how the man got from trashing empty bottles from the bar across the room to standing right behind me. Since this main part of the suite can patch into the hotel's house music, Ed Sheeran is still there to remind me not more than a few seconds have gone by.

"Of... Of course I do." Maybe I can pretend my way back to normalcy. Hell, it's worked for the last hour. We've been a good team, turning rooms at impressive speed. But everything changed back in the elevator, with that single look he bore into me. With that stupid sewing kit he offered. With his charming demand to see into my thoughts. "I mean...it's beautiful." After two more seconds of his expectant silence, I stammer, "Right?"

He pulls in a breath. I can all but hear the gears in his head working. "It's a city," he finally murmurs. "All cities are beautiful in their own ways, I guess. Lights. Architecture. Movement."

"Life." My exhortation has him do a double take. I know it as certainly as I know the lyrics of the song coming from the hidden speakers over our heads. "It's *life*." And it bears repeating, as I take a step closer to the glass. "A collection of lives. Every one of them is a different story, a different dream, a different goal...but all working together too. Meshing and mixing and reaching for something better than what they were the day before, and twining with that same energy in others." I huff out a little laugh. "Oh, God. I just said all that out loud, didn't I?"

"Yeah." His reply, quiet as mine, is filled with a confident husk. I know this because he's stepped over, sliding closer behind me...and now nearly presses up against me. I sigh deeply, fighting not to lean back into his strength and heat. Instead, I focus on his movements, steady as Tulum seas, in the shifting reflection of the tinted glass. "And I could listen all night."

My laugh is nearly a snort now. "You want some butter for that order of corn, mister?"

He shifts a little closer. "Only if bunnies like corn."

*They do. Oh God, they do. Too much...*

"And butter?" Melted to liquid, like the texture of my blood beneath the intensity of his nearness?

"Tell me more." His tone is rougher now. Nearly a lover's bedroom command. Every tingling tissue between my legs confirms it.

*Oh, no.*

I can't start thinking this way.

*We* can't start thinking this way.

But all he's asked for are words.

Words are safe, right?

"It's also...energy." I must sound ridiculous by now, but he didn't flinch from all the quixotic shit I've already spouted, so why not? "A vibrancy, you know? A pace. A collective craziness, I guess. It's something..."

"Something what?" he prompts, filling in my self-interruption.

"Bigger." I go with the first thought in my head...my soul. "It's just...bigger." But what does "bigger" mean to a guy who's been around the world at least a dozen times? "To me, anyway."

The air suddenly feels heavy, probably from the weight of my self-consciousness. I feel stripped and vulnerable. It's not comfortable, but stepping away isn't an option—especially as Reece moves even closer, nearly caging me against the glass with his tall, hard body.

Time for a tactics switch. Big-time.

Snark to the rescue. "Okay, buddy." I pivot, facing him now, turning up a palm. "There are my thoughts. Now pony up the chocolate."

The man isn't deterred. His face is set in serious lines. His eyes are steel gray. "That's important to you, isn't it?" He clarifies. "Living...bigger. Having...more."

"No." I let him see my wince. "Not *having* more." I close my hand, pressing the new fist to the center of my chest. "*Being* more." At a loss for how to explain further, I face the glass again. "There just has to be...something more."

And now there isn't anything left to say. But why does it feel like I haven't uttered anything at all? The air is still too thick, and the new song filling it isn't any help. The Weeknd starts singing—I don't recognize which song, but does it matter when it's The Weeknd?— and my mind starts surrendering even more to the heat of the man pressing closer. I know it before even lifting my head to see him, a beautiful blur reflected by the window, towering over me with sensuous intent.

"There is." His assurance is a warm breath in my hair, a vibrant caress along my nape. "There *is* more, Velvet."

I swallow hard. Fight the shivers coursing down my spine, inching their way toward the front of my torso...into the curves of my shoulders and the tips of my breasts...

"Easy for *you* to say," I whisper. "You've already *had* more."

"Not yet." Aside from a frisson of tension in his shoulders, nothing else changes. He pushes in tighter. Forms his chest to the back of my head, frames his thighs to either side of my hips. And holy wow, what the backs of his fingers start doing to the lengths of my arms...

"Not yet?" I stammer. "What part of 'not yet' are you referring to? Swimming with the sea turtles in Tulum or skiing the Alps at Christmas? Or maybe..."

What the hell was I saying again? I care about that less than the title of the song playing around us, though the lyrics are suddenly magic in my senses. Words of being freed by a simple touch and never having to rush...

"You're my more, Emmalina."

It's pure heat against my neck.

Liquid fire through my body.

Awakened truth in my spirit.

A force I can no longer fight. *We* can no longer fight.

"Oh." It escapes on shaking breath as my head drops, unable to stay upright as this man slings a net of arousal across my whole body. I'm helpless in his snare, muscles going limp and nerves turning to ash, though I still try to fight the pull by slamming both hands against the glass and pushing back. No use, especially as I drag my stare up, only to have my vision filled by our reflection.

*Our* reflection.

One word now. One image now.

Bodies pressed. Breaths mingled. Energies joined. Desires awakened.

"Oh." I have no idea how I'm able to repeat it, or if it even makes sense. "I...I see..."

"Do you?" His growl is almost a visceral vibration instead of a spoken reply, pressed into my neck as he slides his left hand along my arm. When he gets to the end, he meshes his fingers with mine against the window. Our clasp forms a heated cloud of condensation. "Do you really see?" He scrapes the corner of my jaw with the edges of his teeth. "Or should I show you?"

*Yes.* Please *show me.*

"No. Th-That's okay. I-I believe you." I push through the haze of lust, clinging to my last thread of pragmatism. "Reece. We need to... get back to work..."

In my head, it sounds like badass management girl. On my lips, it's more like lusty French maid and worse. The syllables break into breathy pieces as he sweeps his lips up and down my neck.

"Work? What is this strange 'work' you speak of?"

I push out a dry laugh. He doesn't. In the dark world beyond the glass, where our figures still tangle, he hunches over me like a forest beast examining its prey—before deciding the best way to kill it. I marvel at how tiny I look compared to him. How helpless. How stunned. Enthralled by my predator's power...

"Emma," the beast softly snarls. "Emma, *Emma.* How did I go so long without this? Without you?"

That isn't supposed to make it all right.

The goo of my kneecaps tells me otherwise.

I sag against him, startled when my bare backside scrapes the prominent bulge in his pants. How the hell has he hiked my skirt and dropped my panties before I've realized it? And *why* the hell didn't I heed Neeta's advice and not borrow some housekeeping uniform pants for this duty? And what the hell am I doing now, letting myself tremble and whine at the sight of his long fingers against my bare thigh...before he slides them toward my core...

"Oh!" My cry is answered by his growl—and the swipe of his fingers over the hot pearl between my legs.

"Yesssss." He hisses into my ear. "God*damn.* Yesssss."

"*No.* Reece, we—oh, *shit.*" My head falls back as he pinches the most illicit part of me. "W-We can't. I-I'm your—"

"You're my more." He shifts his hand away, encouraging my right knee to settle onto the ottoman he's pulled over with his corresponding leg.

"Regardless, this isn't...and you're—"

"The man who's going to be inside you."

"No. *No.* This isn't right."

"Oh, this is *very* right."

"I *work* for you!"

"All right, then. You're fired."

"Damn it!"

"All right, then. You're hired again."

I'd slap him, if his words weren't so damn true. *This is very right.* My mind resists every syllable, but every cell of my body and instinct of my spirit can't scramble fast enough to embrace it. To seize the gem of desire forged in the caves of fate from the moment we first set eyes on each other.

Fine. So it might be true. Doesn't mean I have to be happy about it.

I pulse my left hand, still locked against the glass by his. He pushes harder, forming his body over mine. I don't want to be happy about how good that feels either. With his chest molded over my back and his face tucked against my shoulder, it's impossible to keep animal tendencies from taking over.

*Ravage me...please...*

"I hate you," I grit out instead.

"I crave you." His stubble burns my neck.

My head plummets again. "I can't want this."

"No." The grate of his zipper cuts the air. "You don't want it." The heat of his groin flares across my ass. "You need it. Like I do."

"Hell." It's a line of bitterness that really isn't, a punch I long to give him but won't—a resolve dwindling faster as he pushes down his pants and briefs, freeing the fire of his erection. He tilts his hips in again, fitting his hot flesh between the swollen lips of my pussy, and I'm certain I've just uttered my own fate. A cock that feels this good can only belong to the devil. And here I am, willingly rocking my soaked center back and forth along that sinful stick. But if this is what hell's like, who needs heaven?

"Fuck." The strain in Reece's voice lends a sliver of vindication. His composure is balanced on just as thin a rail as mine. For a tiny moment, I let myself believe all his words are more than just pretty poetry to get my underwear open. Does it even matter if they aren't? The bastard has gotten his way. My panties are a puddle around my left ankle. My resistance is a few grains of sand washed away by his lusting flood. My senses are tossed like jetsam in the surge—flipped and tossed and drowned until I can't figure out where to come up for air. Every breath is full of his smoky, musky scent. Every heartbeat is synched to the hammering in his chest, pounding against my spine. Every move I make is dialed in to making him swell bigger against my pussy, moan deeper into my ear, grab tighter onto my thighs.

"*Fuck.*" His echo is borne on a chest-deep groan as his body tightens and shakes. His lips are hot and brutal at my ear. "Fuck *me*, Velvet."

I release a shuddering sigh. "Is that a question or a command?"

"You *really* need that answer?"

But once more, we both know that reply, as he grabs my thighs, spreading fingers along my tender flesh and pulling my body harder against his. I shake and moan and gasp, swearing this heat and need and lust are the most intense storm my body's ever been through—and he hasn't even entered me. How is this possible? How is he doing this to me, simply with the scrape of his mouth and the force in his fingertips? His touch is like lightning. His body is like thunder. He's a monsoon around me. A calling to my core...

"Emma. *Emma.*" His voice moves through me, vibrating along my skin and senses. "You..."

"No." I sigh, savoring how our muscles coil together. How our bodies form to each other. "No...*you.*"

His low, lusting breath flows with his long, slow slides. "You... drive me." He works a deep kiss into the bottom of my neck. "You illuminate me."

I shudder and smile as he works his mouth back up to my jaw. "It's my super power."

I swear, just before his short chuckle, I feel a jolt take over his body. But his voice is smooth smoke when he drawls, "It probably is."

"You know what that means, don't you?" I wait one short beat, not giving him time for another comeback. "Now you have to show me yours."

There it is again. The silent but incessant jolt through his frame, covered by another laugh. It's sharper this time, probably because I waste no time in demonstrating exactly what "power" I need from him. Am beyond needing. Am beyond even thinking about. He's turned me inside out. Pulled me beyond my defenses. Taken me to the point of no return. I'm wanton and uncaring, riding my pouting sex along his engorged shaft, lost in a vortex of climbing need and growing fire and pulsing passion.

"Damn. *Fuck*. Emma—beauty—wait. *Wait*. I have to—"

"Hurry," I gasp as he slides his hand from my thigh and fumbles with something behind him.

"Christ." But it sounds more like "rice" because he's tearing a foil packet with his teeth. The next moment, the latex is a cool column between our bodies. As he slides the condom over his length, he dictates, "Say that again. Just like that."

"Hurry." I willingly oblige because one, I mean it, and two, I yearn to make him sound like that again. Like he can't take a breath until I speak again. Like he won't move without my begging gasps. "Please...just...hurry and—*oh!*"

It's a moan of surprise and fulfilment, of pain and pleasure, of joy and sorrow. In his single lunge, I'm finally filled—but as he slides his cock out, retreating until his head teases at my tender lips again, I now know what it's like to be without him. Tears stab my eyes. Everything aches. He hasn't just taught me about the emptiness of my body. He's left me in a deeper darkness. An existence without his passion, his laughter, his energy...

His *more*.

"Reece." I don't care how pathetic it sounds. If he wants to hear me beg, that's damn well what I'll do. "Please. *Please*. I-I need—"

"I know," he husks. "I know."

A moan, deep and dark, pours out of me. He *doesn't* know. If he did, he'd give me more than just his tip, searing at the first few inches of my channel, teasing back into my weeping depths with painstaking seduction.

"But...but..."

"Close your eyes."

I do it because he could ask me to whistle *Mary Had a Little Lamb* right now, and I would. I do it especially because his commanding growl is the sexiest thing to ever enter my body. Okay, the second sexiest.

"Both your hands. Flat on the glass." He pulls the ottoman over a little more, enabling me to reposition my body and comply. "Now both knees up on this."

A serrated snarl leaves him as I obey once more. The new alignment of our bodies seats him deeper, though the penetration isn't close to that first incredible lunge. I need him like that. I need him so far inside, it hurts. I need him to dominate every thought I have, electrocute every cell in my being, fry every circuit in my senses. With every new inch he takes over, my blood sizzles. My skin ignites. My pussy is white-hot from his branding. And still I crave more. I need more...

The lust spreads through me like a virus. I'm fevered with it. Delirious from it. I need relief but never want to be healed. It consumes me, driving every move I make. My limbs writhe and roll, thrusting my channel back over his stalk, a physical plea for his full invasion once more. He answers with sharp, shallow stabs, swirling me into enraged insanity. No. Not insanity. I'm indignant. Enraged. I didn't remotely want this. If we're discovered, he'll be banished to run an ice hotel in Mongolia and I'll never work in this city again. But now that he's turned my body into a raw frenzy, he refuses to give me the right antidote.

"Damn." He grits it as I pump faster. The timbre of his voice is a fireball to my sex, stretching the walls of my restraint, making me cry aloud.

"Please." My fingertips curl against the window. My shoulders snap back, molding against the perfect wall of his chest. He curls around me, draping me in his longing, firing the electrons of our passion even faster and hotter. His thighs are powerful and slick against my ass. He rakes his hands up my arms and slams them on the glass outside of mine. His cock conquers new depths of my body—a piston of such intensity, I wonder if I'm glowing from within. "Please!" I beg again. The piston needs to connect—*now*. The rod needs to strike—*now*.

"*Damn*." His own echo is nearly a groan. "So hot," he snarls. "So tight. I need to be deeper."

"Do it." So finished with begging.

"I don't...know if I can hold it in for much—"

"Then don't." Really, *really* finished.

"It's...been a while for me."

I almost hurl back a glare of disbelief. "You trying to say you're out of practice? Because I call bullshit."

"I'm trying to say...dear *fuck*"—the oath escapes him as our bodies fit tighter—"that I don't want to hurt you, and...*fuck*."

I exclaim the word with him—as his cock takes over everything left inside me.

For a moment, just one moment, we just are. We're locked. Tied by the connection of our bodies, the bond of our breaths, the electrons of the air swirling around us, through us, into us.

It's crazy—at least that's what I try to tell myself—but there's no other way to describe the marvel of the starscape bursting to life beyond my closed eyelids. The sexual race of my body is now the blazing force of my mind, shooting texture and color to my vision. Blue, gold, and silver streaks consume the valley of my passion, colliding so hard that I'm overwhelmed—but when I open my eyes to escape the cataclysm, there's more impossibility for my mind to wrap around.

Are his fingers, still slammed to the glass beside mine, glowing? Is that same indigo hue igniting the crux where our bodies are joined? And why can I *see* every vein in his body as if they've turned into lightning?

"Reece? What the—"

But I can't get the question out. My scream slices the air as he thrusts fully once more.

*Holy. Shit.*

Every inch of my tunnel is invaded, every neuron of my body is detonated.

"It's okay, Velvet. It's okay."

Though his words are hoarse rasps, I believe every syllable. Though all of this is beyond surreal, I accept it. Maybe it's even easier that way. Remembering it as something like a wild dream will make it easier to forget.

Because once we leave this room, I *have* to forget.

Reece's breaths are rough in my ear. He bends one of his knees onto the ottoman, tilting his cock for even deeper plunges. A stunned choke falls out as my pussy flares with pleasure, my eyes squeeze shut, and my senses are lost. The light ribbons are gone. In their place is a solitary glow, a sun into which my senses melt. The heat funnels toward my pussy until the dam of my restraint is nothing but rubble.

And I drown.

Liquid light, all around.

Molten completion, slamming through.

My sex is pure lightning. My senses are raw resonance. My lips open on a soundless scream as the torch inside me brings wave after wave of perfect fire, sparking pleasure so good it's nearly unbearable.

"Reece. *Reece.*"

"Right here." His growl is my ark in the flood, my refuge from damnation. We're a pair of fallen angels, marking a path through the stars with the fire of our fucking. "I'm right here, Velvet."

"Wh-What's happening?" I hear my voice as if through a fog. I sound totally toasted, though the electricity in my pussy counteracts that theory. I'm not drunk. This feels too damn good for drunk.

"I don't know." His grate is filled with just as much wonder. His cock swells at my walls, foretelling his own approach to the cliff of climax.

"You don't *know*?" I'm incredulous. Maybe a tinge scared.

"I've never felt anything like this before."

I believe him but don't want to. Hasn't he felt *everything* before? But as he continues to fuck me, the answer is irrelevant. "Oh," I choke, as new arousal drives my pussy toward a new mountain of awakening. "*Oh!*"

How is this possible? How am I this tightly strung, this stunningly turned-on, once again?

"It's okay." He meshes his fingers with mine, squeezing until it hurts. I welcome his shackles, embracing the pain. It ensures me this is real. Achingly, blindingly real. "It's okay, beauty. Let it happen. Let it take you."

"Says the guy who doesn't *know* what's happening?"

I feel his smile against my cheek. "Then it's an adventure for both of us." He slides his grip along my body, sizzling heat following his fingertips all the way back to my waist. "An uncharted sea." His hold tightens. He controls our pace, ramming my body back over his with faster urgency. Then even faster. "Sail it with me, Emma."

"Yes." No other response makes sense.

"Come with me, Emma."

"Yes!"

We plummet together, descending into our own River Styx, where flames consume us—and then rocket us back to the stars. But now, we don't just zip between the cosmos. We *are* a star, made of light and heat and brilliance, flaring with such force, the supernova is inevitable.

"Christ," Reece snarls.

"Yes." I return the plea.

"I'm going to come." His voice wavers. Something about his moan snags at my senses. "I can't stop," he grates. "God help me."

What's going on? Why does he suddenly sound like he's confessing murder? But even those thoughts vanish as I burst once more, caring only about the convulsions of my walls around his gushing cock.

"Oh," I stammer. "Oh...*oh!*" And though my logic knows there's a layer of latex between our bodies, I swear I can feel every drop of him spill into me. A thousand filaments of energy spread through my sex, as if I've become one of those plasma balls at the geekboy stores at the mall. The sensation intensifies when that electricity branches out, filling Reece's fingers now spread against my hips, as he keeps pumping, rubbing out his scorching conclusion.

"Fuck." He finally breathes against the back of my neck. *"Fuck."*

"We sure did."

My humor is met by Reece's thick silence, pricking a sixth sense in me. Why has the weight of the air doubled in less than half a minute?

Before the next thirty seconds are up, he curls around to swiftly kiss the edge of my jaw before muttering, "I'll be right back." While there's affection in his voice, its twinge of regret still lingers—but by the time I can turn around, he's already disappeared into the bathroom, closing the door with a *whump.*

Confusion hits. It's followed at once by curiosity. Enough to make me surge to my feet, yank my skirt down, and pad across the room. But once there, I hesitate in front of the closed bathroom door. Through the portal, I can hear his pronounced hiss. Then a slippery *fwick*, as he pulls off the condom. He whooshes out a breath. Whispers to himself, "Thank *fuck."*

My forehead bunches. What the hell?

"Errrmmm... Everything okay in there?"

A fast *thunk*—the used rubber hitting the waste can, I assume— before the door is flung back and the man himself fills the opening.

I don't disguise my sharp intake of breath. *By all that's holy.* Probably the *un*holy stuff too. I don't expect this new arrogance from him. Or its crazy effect on me. How can a male wearing his nerve like a second skin, though still covered by every stitch of his clothing, make me want to hump him again already? I can't deny that truth as I take in his sultry smirk, half-lidded gaze, and tumbling hair. His arms are spread, elbows braced against the doorjambs. He crosses one ankle over the other, drawing my gaze downward—to the open V of his zipper and the gasp-worthy body part still bared in that gap.

"Right as rain in here." His gaze matches his tone, alluring and steady. His sultry scrutiny dips down my body. "How about out there, bunny?"

I compel my own composure to stay even, though that means letting my blush run rampant. And no, the irony isn't lost on me. After what I just let him do to me, on the company's time—*his* company's time—my system shouldn't be granting me blush privileges right now. Yet there it is, acutely conscious of his bare crotch. And mine. The skirt might be down, but that stops none of his effect on everything beneath it. I'm wet all over again, my juices tickling as they slide toward my pussy. Reece's stalk, which has never gone fully flaccid, bobs half an inch the moment my arousal scents the air.

"Just...peachy."

Reece curls a smile, making me want to groan. *Holy shit.* The man's generous lips are as mesmerizing as his proud cock. "Peachy, hmmm? Glad to hear that." Just as swiftly, the mirth fades from his mouth...as fresh lust smokes his eyes. "You have no idea how glad."

"Oh, I have *some* idea." My effort at cute and coy is destroyed the moment he reaches over, dragging me close. In the same motion, he finds the top of the zipper at the back of my skirt. Before our bodies touch, he has the enclosure open. As our mouths tangle, the whole garment plummets to the floor. We're flesh-to-flesh once more, my soaked slit cushioning his stiff length, my hungry moan absorbing his harsh grunts. I'm dizzy with disbelief but high on gratitude. How is this even happening? How is my body, my spirit, my very core already so ravenous for him again? This isn't me. At least this never *has* been me. I'm the female with needs beyond my clit. The vanilla-town girl with the kaleidoscope-colored dreams. The one who can count past lovers on one hand and be fine—hell, be *proud*—of that fact.

"Yeah?" But his silken growl has me forgetting all concept of pride, especially as he sweeps me up, parking my ass on the marble vanity top. "Tell me about your ideas, beauty."

His mouth, so elegant and entrancing, hovers less than an inch above mine. He doesn't leave the space empty for long. At once his mouth sweeps down again...then his tongue spears past my lips, demanding a new, wicked dance. Though he leads the tango with smooth mastery, I'm struck once more by his urgent desire, which leads me to actually believe his earlier disclosure. *It's been a while for me...*

"Yours fascinate me more." The words quiver as he yanks me forward, nearly unseating me from the vanity, before wrapping my legs around his waist.

"Uh-uh." His tone is as thunder-dark as his gaze. "Not as fascinating as you, Emmalina Crist." He dips in as if to kiss me again but hovers instead, raking those thunderheads across my face. "I want to know everything about you."

He speaks with such reverence, I don't know whether to be swept away or scared shitless. Then there's the option behind door number three. Total bewilderment.

I funnel all the confusion into a muttered question. "Why?"

He pulls back a little and looks at me with such perplexity of his own, I wonder if he's having second thoughts about this whole conversation—or whatever the hell this exchange is.

But he's still serious, even resolute, as he murmurs, "Why is there gravity, Velvet? Why does the sun come up every morning? Why do stars fall and mountains rise?" He pulls himself closer to me. "Some things are just inevitable." He slides his hips against mine. As he rocks, stroking my clit with the boldness of his cock, I swear his gaze flares with a million points of iridescent light. "Some things are just meant to be."

Well...hell.

Forget fighting the leap of my pulse. The sprint of my heart. The complete swoon of my better senses, turning my I-am-woman-hear-me-roar into I-am-bunny-let-me-melt.

"Meant...to...be." I push out the words between hoarse, heavy pants. "Like the fact that I need you to fuck me again?"

# CHAPTER SEVEN

### REECE

I grin so wide, it hurts.

Fuck. Everything hurts.

Every drop of power in my dick. Every molecule of air in my chest. Every crazy thought in my head.

It hurts, and I've never felt more amazing in my life.

I sure as hell haven't ever spouted such quixotic bullshit and truly meant it. I've never stared at a woman's face like this and sworn I'd never be tired of the sight. And my cock sure as hell has never demanded a repeat trip to paradise this fast after the first visit.

Most remarkably, my hands have never felt like this before.

Yeah...my hands.

They've never ached to hold a woman tighter. Never clenched into fists, fighting back the urge to cradle her face as I kiss her senseless and screw her into nirvana.

And they've never glowed brighter.

Ten garish reminders of the freak I really am.

Which is why I reach beneath us, gripping her ass as I lean in close, consuming her vision with nothing but me as I tell her through my teeth, "Close your eyes, beauty."

The center of Emma's brow pushes into a perfect little V. "Why?"

My jaw clenches. "Emma—"

"You're so beautiful." She delves a hand into my hair. "Let me watch you this time."

"*Close your eyes, Emma.*"

I hate that it jolts her. Hate how it paints her face in nervousness, even though she complies. And I *hate* what it does to her body, tensing her before I can even drag the second condom from my pants.

I want to fascinate her again. Turn her into the mindless she-beast who let me take her in front of the window. Turn her into my partner to the stars.

So once again, I tiptoe into territory I've never traversed with a woman before.

Seduction. The real kind. As in, slow and sensual...and verbal.

"That's good." Simple, but an effective start. Also the truth, though I know everything I'm about to say is the truth. I'm just not sure how. This isn't my normal MO. I've always been a show-not-tell guy. A master in the art of stringing women along with expensive food, expensive booze, and the belief they'll somehow get beneath the suave shell I show the rest of the world.

I don't want to be suave with her.

I just want to be real.

"Yeah. Very good," I say with more confidence. "You're gorgeous like this, Emma." I brush kisses across her eyelids. "No. Not even gorgeous." I swallow and hope she feels it. I hope she knows that texting this shit is one thing but speaking it is another. An experience that makes me feel like anything but a super hero right now. I'm so far out of my comfort zone, I'm in the fucking desert—and she's the only oasis that can keep me alive. "You're...you're gravity." It spills out, lamer than I ever imagined but good because it's straight from my gut. My deepest instinct. "You're morning. And—"

I'm silenced—saved—by her grip around my neck and her mouth jutting up to mine. She shoots her tongue into my mouth. Rolls the gorgeous curves of her hips, drenching my throbbing head in her scorching juices. "And the woman who needs you inside her again," she grates. "*Now.*"

I growl hard. Kiss her harder. There's a charge in our contact now, making her taste sooty but sexy, which awakens an animal drive in my gut as well as my dick. She tastes like *me* and all the places I've already marked her from the inside out. Now I want to find even more.

With that thought dominating my brain, I fumble the condom on. The second it's slammed tight next to my balls, I grip Emma hard and position her for my full, fiery slam. No gradual build-up this time. I'm a rod of rage, full of racing electrons and blazing come, manifested all too clearly by the neon-blue glow cast across her ass. I fixate on that sight, reflected back to me from the mirror, as I plunge deep into her. Faster. Harder. Driving to make her scream. Giving everything to bring her pleasure. Rejoicing in the view of my erection, lunging deeper and deeper into her wet sheath.

Succumbing to her magic.

Giving in to her spell.

Hailing her as my sorceress...as I give her every drop of my own super power again.

## EMMA

Two days after Reece Richards made sure I'd never think of that suite in the same way again, I return to my office from the water cooler, doing my best not to wince. Neeta has come in during my absence and secured herself in the chair on the other side. Privacy is no longer a luxury, so I'm forced to hide how every inch of my ass still feels as if I spent the day at Malibu lazing too long on my tummy, covering everything but my backside.

But that's the boring metaphor for everything that really happened.

For how Reece Richards gripped me so fiercely when fucking me, he left bruises that feel a lot like burn marks.

For how he seared himself into my mind with the same ruthless force.

For how my body has turned pyromaniac on me, craving those flames again.

For how much it hurts to ache for him like this.

And for how much I really like it.

I frown at Neeta, but she's still furiously tapping text into her phone. She glances up as I place my water bottle, newly filled at the cooler, on the opposite end of the blotter from my computer. "If you add vodka to that, I'll steal a swig."

I chuckle, knowing damn well she's joking.

"I'm not joking."

"Okaaaayyy." My deeper frown counteracts the casual blurt. "Sorry, honey. What's going on?"

"You mean what's *not* going on," Neeta returns. "As in, what's happened to Bolt and his hot streak."

I resettle in my chair, jolted again by my private hot streak. "I've been...busy. Haven't even turned on the news. What's going on? Wasn't he just zapping every creep in town with thunderbolts and lightning?"

"Until a day and a half ago, yes." She pushes her sculpted brows together and slides a finger up her screen. "But now he's disappeared into his dynamo den or whatever." She rolls her eyes. "I guess cheese doodles and a *Lone Ranger* binge are more important than saving Los Angeles from rapists, thieves, and vandals."

I huff, progressing to the logical conclusion. "And let me guess. The tour group is now wondering why they bypassed Anaheim to stay here."

"Give the lady a prize." She rings an invisible bell.

With crazy-weird timing, a musical ding erupts from my computer. A window slides in from the left, topped by the name of the person hailing me via our in-house instant message system—set to a privacy level I've never even heard of much less been invited to share.

*Reece Richards*

*Shit, shit, shit.*

I grit my teeth to keep the words from spilling out, but a stressed sigh is inevitable.

Neeta charges. "What? Who is it?"

I shrug, praying I'm convincingly casual. "Rick from housekeeping." Thank God there's a supervisor in that department with an "R" name. If she glances at my monitor, she'll see that much before I close the pop-up. "He thinks the tour group is hoarding the comp shampoo bottles. And he might still be a little peeved about Ree—Mr. Richards and me forgetting to tuck the shams on the beds in the suite during the team turnover."

My message box pings again.

*Emmalina.*

Speaking of tucking a sham.

*Emmalina.*

"Sorry." I flash an apologetic look at Neeta, not having to pretend this time. "I should get this."

*EMMALINA.*

"Of course." Neeta waves an indifferent hand but shows no signs of ceasing her scrolling. Or moving from the chair. "Go ahead. I'm just hoping to find any random mentions of Boltalicious. Maybe he dropped off his hottie leathers for dry cleaning somewhere."

I concentrate on pulling in a fortifying breath but take my time about it. Acting like I'm thinking may actually lead to *doing* it. Besides, the action steadies my fingers on the keyboard.

*You want pompoms with that megaphone, mister?*

A little line beneath my words, looking like a dwindling dynamite fuse on repeat, denotes he's typing a reply.

*Nice segue.*

*Why?*

*Because balls ARE involved with my intentions right now, beauty.*

I had to go and bring up dynamite.
I pass off another long breath as efficient frustration.

*Have fun with those, then. Don't dribble both at once. You may hurt yourself. I have to get back to work.*

My lips twitch. Well, look who just got glib and sassy with the boss. I *am* woman, and my roar is full of sultry power. Maybe *I'll* go out and kick some bad-guy ass.

*You've been at work for four hours.*

My fingers fly, taking advantage of the perfect comeback.

*You only know that because you're still the dictator of my commute.*

*Dictator Richards. Has a nice ring to it.*

*Have fun playing with that one too, your excellency.*

*Four hours, Velvet. By law, you have to take a break.*

Hell.

How is his middle name not *Persistence?* And how does he crash my heart against my ribs by simply messaging that nickname?

I square my shoulders. I *have* to be stronger than this. Remind myself I'm likely not the first woman he's ever called that, no matter how special it feels or how many backflips my stomach insists on subjecting me to. Realize that a rich rogue with eyes like mercury, hair like satin, and the body of a god won't care about the moony-eyed manager he leaves behind once the fascination of the fuck is gone.

*Not relevant. Salaried, remember?*

I preen for a second before clicking send. "Ka. Pow."

While I wait for his dynamite fuse to reignite, Neeta looks up with an inquisitive smirk. "Is Richard being a douche again?"

I send a wry wink. "Nothing I can't handle."

*Take a break, Emmalina.*

*I'm in the middle of something.*

*And it'll be waiting when you get back.*

*From visiting your spire?*

*You like my spire.*

A new huff bursts out. He's right, so damn right, and I can't *let* him be. I really am in the middle of something—and if the tour group is as pissed as Neeta alleges, my work load as Guest Satisfaction Manager is about to get heavier—and I can't even pretend taking a "break" with him will be "relaxing." Peace isn't an option when we're in the same room together, and the more I've pondered it, the more I realize what he said the other night is the only way to explain the wonderful war zone.

There's no explanation for it at all.

Unless stuff like the sun, stars, and gravity are worthy definitions. And they're not.

They can't be.

Which is why I must declare détente now.

*I'm not going to the spire, Reece.*

I send the reply before I can chicken out. And then literally sit on my hands while waiting for his response.

But his typing fuse never reignites.

I tap a toe on my plastic chair mat. The move is actually empowering, giving an excuse to admire the new fire-engine-red pumps on my feet. Okay, so they were the result of shopping therapy as a distraction from *him*, but they're still killer. But even their super powers fade after a long minute of inactivity in the chat box.

I stop the toe tapping. And hold myself back from writing stupid scripts about why he's suddenly fallen off. I imagine him sitting there at his refined desk, in front of those penthouse windows, glorious even in his fury. Who knows what's prompted his silence? The man has a million other things to focus on besides getting peeved with the mousy manager currently serving as his fuck buddy side dish.

*No longer.*

It's for the best that he recognizes that too. That we *both* do.

Blasting aside the lead plate closing over my chest, I minimize the chatbox with an efficient click. "Any luck?" I query, converging my attention back to Neeta. "Mr. Lightning-in-Leather sighted anywhere at all?"

She jerks her head up, tossing her unbound hair across her slumped shoulders. "You mean other than a bad imposter on Melrose, using the lure to flash his junk?"

I groan but finish in a snicker. "So that's a giant no."

"Affirmative, kiddies." With the same wry emphasis, she stabs again at her phone screen. "So we'll probably have the group for just two nights instead of four. *Ugh.*" She turns the device over, slamming it to her lap while letting her head fall back. "That'll teach me to include a last-minute booking on the weekly forecast."

"But you can put a note on the report, right? Explain that the revenue loss was due to circumstances beyond our control?"

She stabs me with a new stare, now drier than her tone. "Last time I checked, a super hero no-show doesn't count as an Act-of-God excuse."

My encouraging smile twists into a grimace. "So who's going to tell Mr. Richards?"

"Says the new teacher's pet herself."

This time, I really need her to be kidding—but I see the

unnerving truth sneaking through her sheepish smile. "Oh, come *on*. Seriously?"

Neeta rises, leaving her phone on the desktop so she can clasp both hands, practically petitioning me. "I'll bring you *ladoo* for the next month."

"Not fair." I've had a weakness for the coconut dessert balls since she shared some with me last week. The girl makes a mean *ladoo*.

"Then consider it a noble act. He likes you, Emma. And you're more comfortable with him than the rest of us."

I double down on the glower. Comfortable isn't how I'd describe the vibe between the man and me, but that justification is way different than everyone else's. They all act like he's a moving nuclear waste zone and they'll start glowing if they breathe around him. And me? I have to keep reminding myself the glow won't last forever.

"And you think that'll make him less ticked about the news?"

"What news?"

It's more dictate than question, issued from the doorway behind Neeta with the authority of an arriving king. The man to whom it belongs is such an image of sovereign glory, I'm shocked there isn't a crown atop his umber waves. That elegant double-breasted suit. That regal stature. That all-encompassing gaze. *I own everything I see...*

I'm actually thankful for my next wave of astonishment. How did he get here from the spire so fast? And looking like he's been at some thousand-bucks-a-ticket gala or awards dinner, instead of giving me shit from his desktop in his dark office?

"Mr. Richards." Neeta really looks ready to curtsy until her nose hits the floor, only I wonder how that'll work in her fitted navy pantsuit. I'm glad I chose a similar ensemble. If I'm not wearing a skirt, the man can't even think of invading his way up it—though the bright silver fire in his gaze leads me to believe he went there for a second. Maybe more than a second.

"Miss Jain." He nods with regal deference. "Have I interrupted?"

"No, no." Neeta's gaze zips back to me, flaring with meaning. "As a matter of fact, Miss Crist was just thinking of calling up to you."

"Is that so?" He jogs a brow, making me wonder if he might really be descended from nobility. The subtext in his eyebrows alone likely sent a few heretics to the guillotine in years past. "What a nice idea. I wouldn't have even had to shout about it."

As I glare, Neeta jolts. "Shout about it? Why?" Again, I wonder if she's about to nosedive for the floor. "Is everything all right? Is there something we can do for you?"

"Nothing I can't take care of myself."

His gaze, gorgeous and dark gray, doesn't leave me.

Neeta's stare, pensive and penetrating, doesn't leave him.

"Okay," she finally says, very slowly—preparing the air for a pause as murky as his eyes.

At last, Reece fully enters the room and refreshes the expectancy in his gaze. "So...Miss Crist? There's something you wanted to discuss?"

Neeta's smile is brilliant, framed by her toffee-shaded lipstick. "Ah, yes. She did."

"I *didn't.*" I burn a meaningful glare her way. "Nothing yet, at least." I gaze back to him. *Whoa.* Even pulling my focus for ten seconds instigates another first-look rush. "Besides, you seem to be having a busy night."

"*Have* had." He shrugs, rumpling his formalwear into even more delicious angles, before clarifying. "Dinner with an old friend. I was on my way up to the office but realized it might be a good idea to check up on things in the trenches."

"The trenches are fine." I insert it before Neeta can formulate anything more. "All systems just grand."

"Outstanding." He unleashes a smile that should be registered as a lethal weapon. Neeta practically simpers. He seems to notice but not notice, if that makes any sense, before stating, "So you won't mind if I glance at the latest guest-satisfaction numbers?"

"Of course not."

"Outstanding." He accentuates every syllable, turning every one of them into aural caresses—so smoothly diabolical in his intent, my senses take a second to catch up. By the time they do, he's already pivoting to Neeta, arms casually folded. "But I'm sure *you* have other duties to attend, Miss Jain. Don't let me keep you."

If my gaze were daggers...

I'd never understood the idiom until this moment, having to pretend the man's suggestion means nothing more than business-as-usual when wicked intent flows like quicksilver from the back of his gaze. Even Neeta picks up on that provocative energy now. Her glances are curious, her shuffle slow, as she turns toward the door. "Of... Of course, Mr. Richards. I'll just be in my office should you need anything, but Emma's been right on top of the satisfaction scales."

His gaze thickens. The edges of his mouth become perfect parentheses for his shit-eating leer. "Satisfaction." He rubs a thumb along his lower lip. "Oh, I've no doubt about that...but really look forward to hearing more."

# CHAPTER EIGHT

### REECE

I follow Neeta to the door and close it behind her. At once, I lock it.

Caging myself in with a killer bunny?

Holy fuck, I hope so. Especially after the goddamned night I've just had. *Dinner with a friend.* Technically, I wasn't lying—if "friend" can be stretched to include the definition "bitch who betrayed me to a gang of scientific madmen and their electronic torture chamber."

I'm ready to forget that now. To put Angelique—and even all those dark months—far behind me. To forget even my super hero style fuck you to The Consortium. As lousy as that'll be for business, it might even do the city some good. Maybe the criminals around here will slither back into their holes instead of attempting fuckery in the name of superstardom.

Fate has offered me something so much better to focus on. Beauty. *This* beauty. The woman willing to hand me her truth straight, even if that story includes her backed-in-a-corner glare as she secures herself behind the desk.

She points at her monitor, now swiveled sideways atop the desk, and then at the chair Neeta just occupied. "You'll be able to see all the reports from there. I'll stay back here."

"If that's the way you want it." I say it with confidence because I mean it—and because she doesn't. She just doesn't know it yet. She still wants to deal with me from her corner. Still insists on putting *me* in a corner. The idea of me, at least. I'm still her safe little box of an explanation—*the billionaire bad boy and his little temporary toy*—and maybe that's not a bad thing. Maybe, ironically, my notoriety is going to serve its greatest purpose of all. Keeping her emotions at a safe distance.

Because I sure as hell don't know where *my* boundaries about this shit went.

Or if they ever existed to begin with.

Just like they're nonexistent now.

I soak up the beauty of her every move, even as she composes herself in her chair again. I watch a long swallow make its way down the side of her neck not covered by her cute side ponytail. Observe, with wicked pride, how a flush makes its way the opposite direction. Her face is so damn gorgeous when it turns that shade of pink... reminding me of how other parts of her body blush so beautifully too...

"How far back would you like to see the reports?" Her voice is crisp and corporate, making my smile inch up again. Does she think the façade will snap me back to some hidden straight-and-narrow? If so, why deflate her? The executive efficiency is ten kinds of turn-on, even causing me to reach and adjust the angle of my cock while she looks to her screen, whisking the little pointer around. "I've managed to get the guest-feedback sheets catalogued going back six months. My goal is to input everything for a year so we can detect trends and throw training toward areas in which we need the most improvement. That being said, I've already noticed a few interesting trends. What?"

She issues the question when finally looking for my feedback and sees I'm actively listening. My elbows are on the chair's armrests, and my hands are steepled in front of my chest.

*That* being said, I'm not going to dick around with pretty words. She deserves better. My truth. At least as much of it as I can give.

"You know I *do* care about those reports, right?"

Her smile blasts through me like an angel visiting hell. "Now I do. Thank you."

And I'm the demon lurking in the caves of that Hades— wondering how long I'll have to wait before she's naked in the flames with me. "But you also know I didn't come down here to go over them right now."

She stops the cursor on the screen before slipping her hand away. She notices that *I* notice, and she clamps her opposite hand over it. "Haven't you had a long night already, Mr. Richards?" Her composure approaches electric aura status on its own as she zips a gaze over me. I can't quite read the source of the energy, either. Nervousness? Fury? Arousal? All three? I'm not sure I even want to know for sure. The mystery is one hell of a hot turn-on. "I mean, seeing how you're all decked out," she babbles, now twisting her hands together.

"Decked out?"

"Yes." She drops her hands while giving me another fast but lusty onceover. Dear fuck, what her attention does to every inch of me... "It's all...more than your usual, I mean," she goes on. "Your tie is so symmetrical, I bet you redid it a few times. That's different product in your hair. It's sleek but stiff, like you didn't want to have to worry about it. You're wearing stiffer shoes. My guess is, they hurt."

Blink. Again. "Yeah. They do."

She blinks as well, though her look is a knowing preen. "Like I said...long night."

For a moment, I don't say anything. It's not necessary when I can boomerang her attitude back, hitching my smirk along for the ride. "Why don't you let me be the judge of how *long* I want to go tonight, Miss Crist?"

Her breath snags. Her cheeks flush, hot and red, as she recognizes how my entendre has just turned the air between us into sensual smoke. I feel my forked tail flicking, my sharp horns growing.

She surges to her feet, bashing me with a tidal wave of the same energy, though one look in her eyes shows me there's an opposite motion in her mind and heart. I should be feeling a thousand kinds of shitty for knocking her on her figurative ass, but right now I've become too obsessed with her real-life backside.

And how sexy-as-fuck she looks, bending over to let me see it better.

And how adorable she is, a bold challenge stamped on her face, as she kicks off one shoe and then the other.

And how astounding she is, with the bottom half of her pinstriped pantsuit already unbuttoned, unzipped, and peeled off.

She glowers at me while draping the garment across her chair and propping one hand on her waist. "Is this what you mean by specifics?"

She marches around the desk, sending a vibe of determined

sensuality that damn near turns my dick into an artisan pretzel. I grunt, the arousal growing from mild distraction to full-on attention, as she strides closer.

"Wasn't my original intent, but..."

"No?" She parks both hands on her hips.

"No." I gulp, fighting to string two logical thoughts together. "I missed you, Velvet. That was seriously it—until the last ninety seconds."

I force-feed the calm into it. Not an easy task. She's making this an impossible discussion to win, though I can understand the intent beneath her accusation. There's been no opportunity to clarify things between us in the last couple of days, especially since I've made it a point to stay out of the fray and let the team do their jobs handling the huge tour group. So now, our interpretation of "teamwork" up in suite 6969—that irony isn't lost on me—has likely been hitting her with what-the-fuck-did-I-just-do-with-my-boss intensity.

In more ways than one.

*Shit.*

She shifts closer, making it possible for me to see the trimmed strip of hair beneath the panel at her crotch. She's not naked, but I crave her like she is. I'm more turned-on than I've ever been with any woman before. Every seasoned seductress I've ever been with...was like eating water crackers compared to the hunger I feel for Emma Crist's rich nectar.

"So, what do you want now, then?"

I plant my feet more squarely and drape both arms along the chair's armrests. Six months of being locked down on a lab table doesn't make it easy for me to relax beneath anyone's control, but

I sense she needs the surrender from me now. Maybe, if I'm lucky, I can even enjoy the fruits of my generosity.

"Hmmm. Why don't *you* supply the answer to that, Velvet?"

Her head tilts. The long gold braid dips into her cleavage. "In what way?"

I breathe in again, letting her gaze linger over the rising tent in my pants. "In any way you like."

She steps closer. I gorge my stare on her curvy, creamy glory and groan deeply as my cock revels in the sight too. My erection is now as painful as it looks, but no way do I want to be anywhere else but right here, right now. My outburst coaxes Emma's stare down. A savoring smile kicks up one side of her lips. God*damn*. A little power looks a whole lot of *good* on this woman.

"Mr. Richards," she finally murmurs.

"Miss Crist."

She tosses her head, flipping the ponytail—and twenty more switches of my lust. It's a playful move, signaling she enjoys the reins I've handed over. The heat in her eyes is the color of burning glass.

I twist my fingers tight around the chair's arms. I slide my hips forward. I clench my teeth. My psyche still isn't comfortable with the change in guard, but my cock and balls don't seem to notice one damn bit.

"All right, then." She comes in a little closer. "Perhaps we can just skip the bullshit."

I feel my stare constrict. "Skip...the..."

"Bullshit." Her echo, and its nod of punctuation, is succinct and sexy. "You know what I'm talking about. The mush. The pretties. The orchids on the appetizer plate. Or, why don't we just ditch the appetizer altogether?"

"Uhhhh..." I grunt as she parts her legs, straddling me. The sound becomes a new groan as she leans in, thoroughly kissing me, sliding her tongue along mine in savoring, lingering possession.

When we break apart, both breathing heavier than before, she delves a hand into my hair and twists hard. "I want to be mad at you."

"Why?"

"Because I shouldn't want this so badly." She pushes in, eyes closing as she drops her forehead to mine. "I...shouldn't want you so much."

"You mean the way I *need* you?" I press meaning into the verb despite my guttural grate. The sound becomes a growl when I slide both hands beneath her blouse, savoring the contact with her warm, soft, pliant skin.

"I have to feel wrong about this."

"I know."

"But I can't feel anything but right."

"I know." I drag her tighter against me. "God*damn*. Emmalina..."

Her damp, warm triangle fits like a custom key against my crotch, unlocking rooms of arousal in my psyche. No. More than that. If I really am this city's super hero, she's my secret weakness. The crack in my shield. The stone to topple my tower. The enchantress driving me to my knees.

Yeah, this very second.

Yeah, to the point that I want to show her that completely... control be damned.

Yeah, as in I suddenly push the chair backward, making it possible to drop to my haunches before her.

Yeah, backing it up by grabbing her ass cheeks to steady her and force her sex against my nose. Her lower body is now in my power. Her armor cracks before my eyes.

*Fuck. Yes.*

Maybe this power swap isn't all one way after all.

"Oh!" She blurts it as I inhale her sexy essence. Such an ambrosia. She's musky honey and silken sweetness, making my mouth water all over the satin triangle. "Oh. Ahhhhh. *Ohhhhh.*"

Her sounds are a symphony of desire playing at crescendo level over her limbs and skin, making her muscles bunch beneath my hands. "Yes." I say it aloud, turning it into a commanding rasp along the seam of her panties. "*Yes,* little Velvet."

"Unnnnhh." She bucks her hips, making it easier to slide my tongue beneath the fabric. "Reece. *Reece.* Wh-What...are you—"

"Enjoying my meal." I savor the vibration of each syllable on her flesh as equally as her reactions. Beneath my questing mouth, she trembles and clenches, shivers and shakes, sighs and gasps. "You did tell me to have at it, beauty."

"This... This wasn't exactly what I..." She trails off, obviously forgetting her words and intention.

"Wasn't exactly what you what?" I don't refrain from the goad, even smirking when she snarls in retort. "What you had in mind when you told me to skip to the good stuff?" I reach in, pulling back the satin triangle, revealing the feast of her secret flesh. "Because Velvet, this *is* the good stuff."

"But...I..."

"Ssshhh. I'm going to enjoy this."

But she only lets me lick a couple of times before protesting,

"This isn't...*ahhhh!*"

"Isn't what?" I grin, totally alpha dog about it, before daring to nibble along her labia. Her little yelp makes the gamble worth it.

She jerks, fighting my ironclad grip on her thigh. "This *isn't* the damn meal."

"Then what is it?"

"This is *you,* making *me...*" She huffs, becoming even more irresistible. "It's... It's—"

"Dessert?" I get in a couple more bites to her pussy. Christ. She's so succulent. So wet. So pink and lush and enticing. "I'm fine with that. Doesn't everyone like skipping to dessert?"

"But—"

"*Ssshhh.*"

"But—"

"*Hush.*"

Technically, her throaty mewl isn't complete compliance— but it's a damn fine substitute. The sound splices the air *and* my bloodstream as I curl in my tongue, unsheathing her sweetest button from its protective hood. The second I touch down on the stiff bundle at her core, she cries out again. I give her more wicked suckles. Her knees give out. I'm ready with my supporting weight.

"Oh, my God..."

I don't bother demanding her silence now. I just guide her into place, directing one of her hands to the desktop and her opposite leg over my shoulder. "I've got you, bunny," I say against her pubic bone before plunging my tongue back into her tangy fruit. "Lean in. Let go. I've got you."

For one incredible second, she does. The rush of her weight, her *trust,* is nearly as good as plunging my dick deep into her channel, and my body tells me so by spurting pre-come into my briefs. I groan from the perfect torment, a sound she takes in all the wrong ways.

"But... But who's got *y-you*?"

Her voice quavers along with her clit, aroused but unsure, as if I've levitated her clear off the floor. She's sure as hell already done that to my senses—and the stiffening rod in my pants seems ready to jump on board with a similar plan. *Levitation for everyone. Fuck, yes.*

"Let me worry about that." I drive it into her wet folds as a command, giving her no option but obedience. Though a strained sound grits through her teeth, her muscles soften beneath my hold. She twists a hand into the back of my scalp and digs her heel into the center of my spine.

"Ohhhhh. Nooooo." Her moans are throaty but high as I greedily tongue her succulent slit, bottom to top and back again, dotting the movement with a determined stab into her tight hole. But not all the way in. Not yet. That moment's coming—and just thinking about it, I'm helpless to hold back my dick from leaking more. It's torture and rapture in the same erotic moment. Nearly unbelievable. Is this going to happen? Is this woman going to make me explode in my pants just from the honor of devouring her gorgeous cunt? She's the juiciest fruit I've ever opened. The sweetest dessert I've ever savored. The most breathtaking woman I've ever pleasured.

It doesn't even matter that I'm not inside her. In so many terrifying ways, she's already inside me.

"Try a new one, Velvet," I growl into her sexy seam. "Try giving me a gorgeous 'yesssss.'"

She obliges the humor in my tone with a warm tug at my hair

but comes nowhere near complying with my suggestion. Which really wasn't a suggestion. I communicate that with a fast bite to the inside of her leg.

"Oh!"

"Don't you mean 'oh, *yes*'?"

"You have got to be kid—*oh*!" Another bite, this time to the top edge of her clit, makes her jerk back by a couple of inches. I don't let her get farther than that. "Oh my hell," she rasps. "Oh my—oh *Reece...*"

It's not the first time in my life a woman has panted those words to me—so why does it feel like the first? Why am I zapped with awe I've never felt, surged with more power than I've ever celebrated? The logical grab is there in front of me, that my cock has been so direly neglected for a solid year it's now leading the parade for the rest of me, but that's the desperate—and inaccurate—way out. This singular desire, for this sole woman... It's more than drought-recovery dramatics.

But how much more?

I'm not the same man I was a year ago. Angelique's "friends" altered the color of my eyes. The length of my legs. The resiliency of my muscles. The very chemistry of my blood. How much of me is *me* anymore—and is *that* the part falling so completely for this woman? Or are all these sensations courtesy of the new me, the phoenix from the ashes? If that's the case, what do I even know about him or what he's able to give a woman like Emmalina?

A woman who wants more. Who deserves more. Who deserves everything.

An everything neither part of me will be able to give her in the long run. Because eventually, if all goes according to plan, I'll be dead.

But right here, right now? Giving her ultimate pleasure? Working my lips to untwist the most mind-shattering climax she's ever known?

That I can do.

That, at least, hasn't been electroshocked out of my consciousness.

I summon it all back to my will. Use every erotic trick in my wheelhouse to bloom her, spread her, arouse her, entice her. I even slick my tongue across her with new flicks and strokes, emboldened by her mewls, moans, pushes, and prompts. The more responses she gives, the more engrossed I become. My world becomes the heady trembles of her thighs, the lush opera of her breaths, and the perfect vibrations of her cunt, enticing me to explore deeper...deeper...

As I do, making my cock harder. *Harder.*

"Holy. *Shit.*"

A stream of her honey fills my mouth. Yeah. *Fuck.* So damn good.

"Reece!"

She blurts the protest after trying to pull away, but I yank her even closer. With my hands cupped to her backside, I'm able to hide my glowing fingertips in the crack of her ass. Double win? The motion spreads her sex from behind, warming her pussy for the new invasion I'm about to launch.

As she keens a little higher, I moan a little deeper. Her thighs bunch and buck. Her ass squeezes and squirms.

"I-I thought you wanted to fuck me."

"Oh, I did," I growl. "And I will, Velvet...believe me."

I feel the conflict take over her—possibly preparing for me to stand up, slam her to the desk, and ram into her. Ramming *does* happen, courtesy of my tongue speared into her tightness.

She fists my hair. Her grip slips on the desk. Pens, papers, and a tumbler of water crash onto her chair as her gasp shudders the air.

I don't relent.

She needs this.

I can feel it in every inch of the plush walls clamping over my tongue, urging me farther inside her trembling, tight body.

*I* need this.

My cock, getting relentless friction from the trap of my pants, broadcasts the update with throbbing clarity. My balls bellow their second on the motion, ignoring my efforts at readjustment. It's no longer a matter of *if* for those fuckers; it's a matter of *when*—though I'm pretty sure of the answer to that query already.

I'll blow when she does.

And fuck, how she does.

"Oh...*wow*." Her voice is shaky and hoarse. Her body is tense and trembling. Her pussy is hot and soaked. "Oh, Reece. I'm...I'm..."

Her words dissolve as her body takes over, communicating the rest. The second she throbs around me, drenching my tongue with the cream of her climax, my balls blast an inescapable fire up my cock. I explode too, horrified but a little giddy. I've come like a wild teenager—from the bliss of bringing *her* pleasure.

It feels good. So fucking good. And unsettling. And terrifying. So much so, I'm frozen in place for a long moment.

Fuck.

I just got off—literally—by putting someone else's needs before mine. This isn't a shred of anything I recognize, not even a drop in the ocean in which Lawson Richards taught me to survive a long damn time ago. On Dad's ship, only one motto mattered. *Every man for himself.* The patriarch himself values it so much, it's why I haven't been blackballed from the family altogether. Secretly, my douchebag rebellion pleased the bastard. I possessed the spine neither Chase nor Tyce had ever seemed to grow—which, before my spectacular fall, was probably why I took the behavior to such epic heights.

Or was it?

If my life hadn't wound down this exact path, I never would have arrived here at the most extraordinary epiphany of my existence. At a moment that is making more sense than all twenty-seven years before it. At the feet of the person who's brought me here.

The woman for whom I've fallen. Literally. Wholly.

The creature who crumples gently to the floor with me now, shuddering in the last throes of her climax, sagging into my arms with kitten-like surrender. I swear she starts to purr as I circle soft fingertips along the back of her neck, their soft glow illuminating the stray strands of her ponytail. With a resolved breath, I'm able to dial back the lightsabers of my fingers even more. Only my nailbeds pulse now, pulsing in time to my heartbeat. I work on calming that pace, but it isn't easy with her face consuming my attention... With the satisfaction, a glow of its own, of knowing I alone brought that sated serenity to her incredible face.

After a few minutes of our peaceful silence, she releases a long, soft breath. "Mr. Richards?"

"Yes, Miss Crist?"

"We have to stop meeting like this."

"Couldn't agree more."

Her eyes flash open. Her pupils are huge and aqua—and alarmed. "Really?" A new flush takes over her face. She hastily clears her throat. "I mean, of course you agree." She sweeps a look over her nude lower half. "This *is* getting kind of ridiculous."

"Agreed once more." I feel a little shitty for leading her thoughts on, but only a little. Sometimes the endgame justifies the play. Only by throwing her off guard can I pry more edges from her armor, exposing her to see—and feel—the importance of what we've begun here. "I'd even say it's gone beyond ridiculous."

"Well." She stiffens and attempts to straighten. "That's good, then—"

"Oh, I wouldn't call it good."

"Pardon me?"

I wrap an arm around her waist, preventing her from completing her frosty escape. I melt the rest of her iceberg with a thorough kiss, not letting go until she opens for the dominion of my tongue. By the time I pull back, she clearly craves more. Good. She doesn't get any quarter from my gaze, which I keep latched to her while spreading my other hand along the back of her head.

"Yeah," I utter, my breath ragged. "Beyond ridiculous. Which means you don't get to bring any reports or furniture dusters next time."

"Huh?" Her eyes flare. I'm torn between grinning at her and just kissing her again. "Wait. *Next* ti—"

"Which will *not* be two nights from now. As a matter of fact, I won't settle for *one* night."

Her brows crunch. "Reece, what are you—"

I kiss her into silence. It's quick and fast this time, because my point still isn't complete. "What am I?" I counter. "What I *am*, Emmalina, is fed up with this. With us, and our treatment of this."

"This?"

"Yeah. This. Us."

Her armor breaks away a little more. She quirks her lips upward, and her eyes shimmer like we're standing in full sun. "There's...an 'us'?"

Hearing her repeat the word drops a massive weight on my chest—with only one possible phrase to set myself free. "There is now."

Yeah. *Oh, yeah.* That's perfect. That's right.

In my new lightness, I tenderly brush my lips across hers. "But that doesn't mean we have to define anything other than now." The honey of her mouth is so damn tempting. "No projections or forecasts. No definitions or boxes. Nobody telling us what we are or aren't. Just this. Just the magic. Just us, okay?"

She releases a high, soft sigh. "Okay."

"But that also means one more thing." I tug her hair harder, enforcing her attention. "I refuse to fuck you on another floor, footstool, or any other furniture not designed for being naked and horizontal."

She curves her lips again. *So goddamned gorgeous.* "Okay."

I tug again. Her amenability makes me want to push my luck. "So when you get off shift tomorrow morning, you're coming straight up to the penthouse."

Her grin grows. "Okay."

"And you're letting me make you breakfast."

*Here's* where her grin fades—though not enough to make me stressed. Not yet. "Breakfast." She cocks her head. "So is that before or after the naked and horizontal part?"

I kiss her again. I can't help it. Resisting her is like denying myself the privilege of breathing. There's tongue involved too. Lots of it. And hair pulling—hers *and* mine. And groping, twenty fingers' worth, as we feel and fondle and grab and possess, sealing the new bond between us in the most primal, perfect way possible.

# CHAPTER NINE

## EMMA

I emerge from my office, but I'm still in a fog. A giant, pink-tinted bank of the stuff—and for once, I don't fight. I'm like one of those cartoon girls with birds and stars swirling around my head—or in the anime version, with my pupils turned into bulging hearts. Maybe that's a good thing. If everyone's gawking at my eyes, they won't notice my knees have turned to taffy—another write-off, considering I don't need them anymore.

Knees aren't important when a girl can just float through life.

Okay, not *Life,* capital *L.* It's only *life* right now, all lowercase. It's not like Reece marched into my office and shut and locked the door with a ring in his hand.

Though the man did show how magical he can be on his knees...

And incredible. And passionate. And giving. And bold.

Stealing my breath. Demanding my surrender. Blowing my mind.

Yeah, even now. *Especially* now—a comprehension that has me gripping the frosted-glass countertop at the front desk for support. I actually glance down, confirming I'm truly and solidly planted, though the pastel cloud still lingers. The stratosphere into which Reece Richards launched me with the power of one word.

"Us."

I run a finger along my lips after whispering it. I can feel the contact, meaning this must really be my life. Not a dream. Not a bizarre alternate world in which Reece Richards isn't a tabloid darling and a world-class rogue and hasn't just snuck out of the executive offices in the back elevator with a dorky smirk on his lips and my Pentatonix tour sweatshirt tied around his waist—hiding the crotch he's just soaked while pleasuring me.

Holy *wow*, that pleasure. Right before he brought on the wizardry. The sincerity. The honesty.

The word that changed everything.

"Us." I dash it off again, almost in a song, while clicking into the guest-services log from one of the front desk terminals. Fershan is also at the desk, though he's talking on the phone at the other end. Observing the lobby is busier than usual, probably due to the bored tour group members deciding to drink their night away in the bar, I stay put in case he needs any backup. Besides, a good song starts playing. A classic. My spirit as buoyant as the tune, I start quietly singing along with the anthem.

"I got me a Chrysler, it seats about twenty, so hurry up and bring your—"

*"Excusez-moi, mademoiselle?"*

I shut off my metaphorical microphone somewhere between "jukebox" and "money" before stammering, "Yes? I mean, good evening, ma'am. I'm so sorry. I was pulling something up, and then—"

"Singing?" The blonde, a stunning mix of classic Catherine

Deneuve and Gwen Stefani, adds to the exotic factor with her French accent. I gawk a little longer as she lifts one side of her flawless crimson mouth in a droll smile. "What would the world be without songs, *n'est-ce pas*?"

"Valid point." My response is polite but guarded. Why is this creature, in her black cashmere dress and red-to-black ombré fingernails, making my skin prickle and my instincts edgy? Okay, besides the obvious—that she's worldly, sophisticated, and oozes more sexuality from one of those tapered fingers than I do in my whole body. This is the case for nearly half the women I meet up here, so that doesn't fly in this instance. There's something else about her. An aloofness but a watchfulness...

"How can I be of service to you this evening, *Madame*—"

"*Mademoiselle*"—she dips her head, smoothly deferential about the correction—"La Salle." A smooth arc of her hand produces a business card that wasn't there two seconds ago. The engraved header gives away her first name. *Angelique.*

Of course.

A name evoking the heavens for a woman who could tempt a dozen monks to sin. At the same time.

"International Commodities." I read the next line down. The only other text on the card is her phone number, prefaced by the international dialing code. There's no company name or her specific position in that organization—though for some reason, I'm anxious to find out. Or perhaps she makes me anxious, period. "Sounds... cosmopolitan."

"In a manner of speaking."

"What kind of commodities, if I may be so bold?"

"Collectibles." Her tone remains impassive. "Rare finds. Objects of wonder. Works of art."

She moves at last, angling an elbow up to the counter, drawing out the last of it with curious vocal emphasis. *Worksss of arrrt.* All too clearly, I realize she isn't talking about Renaissance busts and oil paintings of virgins getting pounced by devils—though this makes me feel exactly like one of those hapless maidens, gazing toward a heaven that doesn't care about the Lucifer about to rape her.

And did I seriously just go there?

This is what I get for skipping my protein bar and yogurt to let the boss feast on *me.* My brain's turned cannibal on itself, eating valuable logic links. But a logic deficit is still no reason to be rude.

"So how may I assist you, Mademoiselle La Salle?" Again, I take in her ensemble. The cashmere is luxurious and fits her toned curves flawlessly. She wears no accessories except for diamond drop earrings so brilliant they must be real. More bling flashes from her feet, adorned in a pair of peep-toe platforms with black insets. "Ground transportation, perhaps?" I dare a between-us-girls grin. "You haven't dressed up like this for the crowd in the bar. Who's the lucky guy you're going to meet?"

Her laugh is an elegant husk. "You mean...already *have* met."

"Ohhh." My voice rises knowingly. "That explains a great deal."

"*Comment ça?* A great deal of what?"

"Of everything." I nod toward her. "Here in LA, we call it your vibe...your energy. The French probably have a more melodic term."

"*Je ne sais quoi?*"

"Sounds about right." I'm able to smile and mean it, but when she responds with nothing but a silken silence, I'm back in the realm of the gawky nerd trying to chat it up with the prom queen. "Well, then. It's clear that you're a woman who enjoyed her evening, at least."

"Hmmm." She leans a little closer, still looking like a cat contemplating a bowl of cream, until I even get the impression she's smelling me. "That likely depends on how you define enjoyable." Her gaze, wide and inquisitive as a Siamese, lifts to my blushing face. "Perhaps *you* have had some 'enjoyment' tonight as well, my friend?"

Heat floods my face. The woman's smile widens. I wave a dismissive hand. "I'm...working."

"Hmmm," she drawls again, one brow arching in perfect amusement. "Of course." She smoothly folds one hand atop the other and rests them on the counter, the move of a feline Bond girl in one of those scenes where you don't know if she's a good girl or a killer. "So I am just...imagining...that interesting scent of yours, then?"

I'm validated but weirded out in the same strange moment. She *is* sniffing. "I only wear light body spray to work. Maybe that's strange in your circles, but it's common courtesy in mine."

"Ah. Of course." She backs away, dipping her head. "*Desolée.* I meant no intrusion. It is only that..."

"What?" I'm more irritated than interested now. The only creature fascinated by a cat's string is the cat—except her teaser has a chunk of psychological Godiva tied to the end. I only hope the chocolate isn't laced with arsenic.

"*C'est rien.*" She quirks another half smile. Zero sincerity backs the look. "It is nothing."

I return the look, probably with more gusto than I should. Hanging with the high-end circles of the OC, where every other pretentious person irked me, honed my perfection at the skill. *Kill 'em with kindness—and if kindness isn't possible, fake it.* "So how *did* you need our services tonight, mademoiselle?"

"Ah." She dashes a finger up, and I almost expect to see a reminder string tied to it. Instead, she opens her graphic-print Balenciaga and produces a pair of items much nicer than string. The cufflinks are simple but luxurious, squares of silver inset with black diamonds. They're the kind of thing a man would never buy for himself but would wear with pride if given from a special woman.

"Ah." I repeat it with meaning—and more than a little relief. Deneuve has a weak spot after all. "These are stunning."

"*Merci.*"

"And...the man for whom they're intended?" I go there, but with care in my voice.

"Equally as stunning."

Just like that, my relief disappears—though I don't return to unnerved either. I'm...confused. Her words don't match the vibe from her eyes. *Je ne sais quoi* has gone *au revoir.*

"Unfortunately, we were caught up in a...discussion. He left them behind in the car."

"Well." I try to focus on my monitor, clicking to the in-house guest registry instead of gawking at her mysterious expression. No luck. She's weirdly riveting. Not a trace of a smile touches her lips, though her longing is a palpable force on the air. "That must have been an epic discussion."

"They usually are with him."

*It's none of your business, Emma.* Mademoiselle La Salle and I have already skated on the edge of too much information with each other.

"And his last name?" There. Cordial but impartial, likely what she's been after this whole time anyway. "So I can call up to his room for you," I clarify. "Or, if you prefer, I can just store them in the hotel's safe and leave a message in his room."

Another win for professionalism—until the woman picks *that* moment to break the surface of her cream, erupting in a light laugh. "Room? Oh, he is not a *guest* in this hotel, *mon amie*."

My face tightens into a scowl and a vise closes over my chest. "He...what?" I manage to ask, despite my instincts suddenly clicking and knowing what her response will be. And dreading it.

"*Non*." The worldly smile slides into place. "He *owns* this hotel. You know him, *oui*? Monsieur Richards?"

I'm rocketed out of my fog, only to descend into another. A darker mist. No more cotton-candy clouds. Sherlockian gray and Jack the Ripper black are the new colors of my vision, shrouding my movements.

Somehow, I manage to make an excuse—more truth than *she* needs to know—that I'm suddenly not feeling well. I hand her off to Fershan and stumble away. *Far* away. A black corner. An empty office. Somewhere with space for my shock to choke out, the *shit-shit-shits* to fade, and the nausea to pass.

Or maybe not.

"Em? Dearie?"

Neeta finds me in the copy room, butt parked atop the shredder, head between my legs over an empty trashcan. Returning to my office is nowhere near an option, not after what I just did in there with Reece.

After what he did before *that* with Angelique La Salle.

*Us.*

His perfect spell of a word.

Did he use it with her too? Before or after she got him out of those cufflinks? Taking off the cufflinks meant she'd gotten him out of his shirt. I've never even seen the man without his shirt. But there I was just an hour ago, two offices away, letting him "us" me into visions of pink castles, swirly stars, and omelets cooked in his decadent designer kitchen.

The comprehension brings back the fog. And the sick.

"*Dearie.*" Neeta crouches next to me, voice resonant with concern. "What is it?"

"I don't know." Not a lie. Have I known Reece Richards at all? Were *naïve* and *desperate* plastered that clearly across my forehead this whole time? "It just hit me." I'm more sickened when realizing *his* lie from earlier in the week now provides my perfect alibi. "Maybe I never got rid of the other bug that bit me."

Neeta's features tighten. She shakes her head. "And both times, you had to spend time with Reece Richards."

I push out a long huff. "He's not a Zika mosquito, woman."

"But he's just as strange." She shakes her head. "Gorgeous but strange."

"I refuse to validate this conversation." That's the truth too—though it's also a convenient cut to the real issue at hand. "I... I think I just need to go home."

*I need to be anywhere but here.*

In an environment *he* can't control. A place where I can think. More to the point—where I don't have to think at all.

"Of course." She starts, glancing at the clock. "But it's nearly eleven. Will you be all right on the train? Maybe I can spare Fersh or Wade to drive you..."

"The hell you can." I inwardly applaud myself for always insisting Z drop me around the corner from the lobby. I also know he's already waiting in the same spot, which is perfect. My route to the train station is the opposite direction. But I don't care anymore. Or feel the need to answer to his "employer" about anything.

It's oddly comforting to get onto the train again, especially at this time of night. Rush hour is long over, giving me space to breathe along with the comfort of anonymity. The roar of the ride is perfect too—a fitting sparring partner for the rage of my senses, the tumult of my heart.

The Purple Line ends at Union Station, and I walk to the platform for the Gold Line with my head down and arms tucked in. It's a warm evening, with summer tickling the early June air, but I can't stop shivering. As much as I hate being cold, I welcome the chill. I don't want to be warm right now. Don't want to even think of the last time I was warm, just an hour ago.

A lifetime ago.

A heartbreak ago.

I'd been giggling at the sight of Reece's ass wrapped in my sweatshirt, along with his sheepish smirk. He'd asked how I'd like my eggs. I'd responded, "Hot and firm—like your fine ass, Mr. Richards."

He'd grinned like a loon and told me I'd earned champagne with breakfast too.

I wonder how Angelique likes her eggs. I wonder if she earns herself champagne too.

The train arrives. I stumble onto it as the tears hit again.

By the time I stop, I'm honking gobs of snot into a tissue—and realizing I've bawled my way through three stops. Going the wrong damn direction on the line.

After groaning in three different octaves, I glare up at the salsa ad mounted over the door. It features three parrots in mariachi outfits, complete with little ornate vests and sombreros. I can see the humiliation pouring out of their little birdy eyes. "Been that kind of a night for you guys too, eh?"

I hurry off at the next stop. The train pulls away, leaving me alone on the platform to wait for the line going the correct direction. Not entirely alone, if I count the family of opossums scuttling in the shadows next to the tracks.

A gust of night wind howls through the station. The chill in my bones seeps deeper, prompting me to head for the shelter of the empty exit stairway. It could be fifteen or twenty minutes before I see another train, and I miss my sweatshirt for more practical reasons now.

"Think warm." My mutter is low, rough, and miserable. "Think Palm Springs. Think hot bubble bath. Think Malibu in July."

Yeah. Malibu. My go-to for long afternoons with my beach chair, a book, and a can of Cactus Cooler. The drink is one of my guilty indulgences, a holdover of childhood memories before we moved to the land of green tea and vitamin water. Bright orange drink. Glittering blue ocean. Brilliant cyan sky. So bright, it hurt to look at the horizon. So bright and silver...

Like Reece's eyes.

*No.*

I refocus, thinking more about Malibu. The powerful rush of the waves countered by their gentle fizzle on the shore. Might and mist...

Like Reece's voice.

"*No*, damn it."

It's barely more than a grunt, but it echoes through the stairwell like a shout. In reply, the air just gives me more ghostly wind...

And then a quiet laugh.

And another one.

Arms still crossed, I whirl around and peer across the station. Still nothing but the opossums.

I whip back toward the stairway.

And come face-to-face with three leering gazes.

Men.

Okay, boys—though they swagger and stare and salivate like men, taking me in like a pack of hungry wolves surrounding a rabbit. I attempt a polite nod—while backing away. All three of them step with me. One of them moves farther, sliding around to my other side.

"Good evening, gentlemen." I try to give them the benefit of a doubt. Who am I kidding? It's for my benefit too. I can't allow my fear to buy into the intentions I sense behind their eyes. It's true, right? What they say about predators being able to smell fear? With that thought in mind, I tuck a hand into my purse. "My hand is on my mace, so let's ensure I don't have to use it, all right?"

I'm so busy being calm, I never take a moment to tack on vigilant—demonstrated when my purse disappears off my arm. The whole thing is tossed across the stairwell except for the mace can, which flies twenty feet as the middle creep moves in, slamming me against the wall. He's also the largest, with sizable muscles under his track pants and plaid shirt.

"We'll show you how to use shit, all right." He slides a greasy kiss to my cheek while the third guy scoots in, breaking open the fastening of my pants. My heart clutches and my breath halts as he uses the tip of a knife to slice the fabric open the rest of the way. "And if you're quiet and pretty, we won't have to show you how Freddie likes using his blade in other ways, either."

"She *is* pretty," the first one croons. "I like her, man."

"Bitch is gonna be good," says Freddie, twirling his knife. "I can tell. Called us gentlemen and everything. Hey, we should even use condoms."

*Shit-shit-shit-shit.*

*Help-help-help-help*!

The pleas pound my spirit in time to the frantic air that's cycling between my lungs and nostrils. The asshole handles the knife with enough fearless finesse that I know he's used it on human flesh before. That he won't hesitate to do the same right now. Wasting my strength begging for mercy isn't viable either. The guy's stare is jacked with enough insanity and arousal, I'm sure he'd enjoy my pleas—and my pain. He backs up the theory by barely flinching when his tall friend kicks him in the shin.

"Fuckface." The big one grunts. "We used our last ones on that little thing with the pink hair in Santa Monica last night."

"Ohhh yeah. Sorry, man. I was baked."

"Like you are right now?"

"Hmmm. Maybe."

"*Pffft.* That settles it." The first guy drops the front of his pants. "I get to go first. Freddie takes forever when he's high, and I'm not waiting like I did last night."

"Yeah?" Freddie retorts. "And what did you have to lose? I nailed her good and hard. Lubed her for you, dickhead. Wasn't like we had to worry about Boltalicious poppin' outta the woodwork."

The comment primes my tears, making me acknowledge the thread of weird hope to which I've been clinging—that someone, anyone, will come along with both the guts and the force to prevent this from happening. But the Lone Ranger is just a comic book character, and *Boltalicious* is on his mysterious do-gooding break—meaning this *is* going to happen.

I squeeze my eyes shut, hoping it'll happen with me still in one piece at the end.

Too late.

Physically, I'm still whole. Mentally, I've already started to detach. *Survive.* The goal stamps on my mind, my beacon in the darkness of what these monsters prepare to do.

Tall Boy laughs, cinching my hands even tighter. He moves to the side, which angles his armpit over my face. I struggle not to breathe, an impossibility given the new force of my tears. Stenches assault my senses, each of the odors at least three days old. Grease, motor oil, sweat, pot—and those are the elements I *can* identify. A few others are nasty mysteries, for which I'd likely be grateful if I could feel anything except terror. "Ha. Good one, cuz," he says. "Boltalicious. That shitpile's as ragged as a wad of chewing gum anyhow."

"Pretty on the outside, gooey on the inside?" The creep still playing with his penis drawls it.

"If *I* ever got to mix it up with the guy? Shit yeah. I'd expose that hustler for what he really is. Penny pranks, special effects, and low-budget magic tricks."

He pauses, but only for a second. Encouraged by his friends' snickers, the asshole clearly has more to say.

Until he doesn't.

The air is blasted, sucked, and moved around us with such violence, all four of us are toppled to the concrete floor like a rug has been yanked from under us.

*Whomp.* The guy who was just pinning me is slammed back up against the wall. His arms and legs splay out, pinned in place by giant invisible thumbtacks. That's the only way I can describe it. The asshole squirms, fighting bonds that aren't there, incredulous shock claiming his face just before a wet splotch appears at the front of his jeans.

The force of nature that put him there steps out of the shadows surrounding the tracks.

A badass in black leather. Hybrid ninja boots. Maserati mask. Lips curled in fury.

"Abracadabra, motherfuckers."

## REECE

Thank fuck this isn't one of those gigs requiring me to get it right on the first try. Because right now, I'm a super hero with completely screwed alignment. As in, enraged-to-the-point-of-impaired screwed.

After three failed attempts that resulted in two of the three jerkwads bonking around the station like pinballs at the mercy of a maniac, I finally succeed at my original intent—knocking them together hard enough to land them in the same unconscious heap. That being done, and after vowing to send a check to LA Metro as penance for crashing them into five lights, two vending machines, and several support pillars, I wait for the calm to settle in. I force deep breaths in. Back out. Concentrate on loosening my fists. No use. Fuck me.

I raise my head, getting a glimpse of myself in one of the chrome tube railings, and am stunned I'm not the color of glowing broccoli. On paper, my reaction makes sense—but the daggers chopping up my gut aren't garden-variety fear. This shit is terror, stark and sick, spawned the moment I got back to the penthouse and obeyed a gut instinct to check the security cams in the executive-office hallways. Watching Emma all but crawl out of the copier room while leaning into a clearly concerned Neeta pricked my first alarm. The shit clanged to five alarms once I clicked to the front desk feed—in time to watch my preening ex-girlfriend making nicey-nice with Fershan Bennett, my cufflinks in her hand.

*Those damn cufflinks.*

Yeah, the ones I haven't been able to even look at for a year, so deep and Pavlovian is their hold on my memory. On my fear...

Fear not rising to half of what struck when I comprehended the scope of Angelique's game—resulting in Emma leaving her shift and fleeing the Brocade.

Running from me.

In the middle of the damn night. In the heart of downtown LA.

Into the very situation I've been paying Zalkon to help avoid. But this isn't his fault. This is my shit to own. My mess to fix after thinking a neutral meeting with Angelique wouldn't end up with the woman trying to keep me on her hook, no matter how dirty her tactics.

Like showing up at the front desk of my own damn hotel and smearing that dirt on the one person who never deserved it.

Garbage I'll have to clear from my life another day.

Right now, I've got other nonrecyclables to worry about.

Fortunately, two of those chunks are down for the next few minutes. Now to deal with the Grand Poobah trash daddy.

"What the *hell*?" the blow stick yells. I let him dangle, getting a firsthand taste of my "penny pranks" with his ass still flattened to the wall. Indulging a sadistic streak, I focus another electric pulse south of his waistline. He screeches as I push the energy harder, crushing his balls like a device in a BDSM dungeon, turning his erection into a raisin. "Wh-What are you doing?" he gasps. "Come *on,* man. Th-That's my *junk,* dude!"

"Couldn't have said it any better myself, *dude.*" I twist my wrist the other way, giving his 'nads a new spin on the Blue Balls Tilt-A-Whirl. "Stop whining. You'll be back to normal in two or three weeks."

"Two or three *weeks*?"

I shrug. "Give or take. Though, keep sticking that shit into places it's not welcome, and I'll be back up your ass, turning it into permanent pieces for the county scrap heap." Finally, I yank back the magnetic field, letting him crumple to the floor and tuck into full fetal. "We copasetic on that?" When all I receive is a hurried nod, I take a step closer. "Sorry. Speak a little louder. We 'hustlers' have shitty hearing."

"Yeah," he finally grits. "We're copasetic."

I nod, though I'm hardly relaxed. Now the difficult part of the night. Turning to Emmalina—and communicating Reece's message using *Bolt's* persona.

As soon as I face her, I'm shocked but not shocked. Yeah, this is going to be hell to pull off—but for reasons I hadn't foreseen even from miles away.

As always, her beauty temporarily sucks out my breath. Even now, with her hair a brilliant tangle, her cheeks streaked with makeup, and the front of her pants slashed open, she mesmerizes me in ways I can't describe. Flips exclusive buttons. Wakes primitive urges of possessiveness. I want to haul her close. Inhale her until I breathe nothing else. Kiss her senseless, and then ban her from ever taking the goddamn train again.

Not a possibility anymore—but not because of the façade I have to keep up. Because of all the shields *she's* had to drop and her estrangement from the creature she's bared. A woman who gapes at me, eyes as wide as always, but in fear instead of wonder. Who trembles in a rush of night wind but recognizes her chill extends far beneath her skin's surface. Who opens her mouth, trying to form words, but only croaks helplessly—and clearly hates herself for it.

Lost, and visually pleading with me for answers, she closes the distance between us with three faltering steps. As she grabs onto me, red-rimmed stare not leaving me, she rasps two words that stab to the center of my gut.

"You're...real."

I nod, wondering why I suddenly feel like the mirage to her

desert traveler. But I'm not the one who vanishes. Her eyes roll to the back of her head, and she goes unconscious in my arms.

With a soft, sublime smile on her face.

# CHAPTER TEN

## EMMA

I'm smiling.

I know it before I even open my eyes.

It's puzzling, because I know I'm not even in my own bed—*am I even in a bed?*—though right now, none of the "important" details seem to matter. I feel like I'm waking up from novocaine. Something should hurt, but I don't give a damn. I may not give a damn again. Everything's soft and quiet and smells so freaking good...

I roll over. Whimper a little. *Okay, ugh.* The earlier question? About what should hurt? The answer is *everything.* Have I been hit by a truck?

I amend that assessment the second my eyes are open.

If it was a truck, it knocked me to a damn beautiful spot. At first sight, I wonder if I'm back in the penthouse at the Brocade. The view is just as sweeping, with the beginnings of dawn sifting through the maze of city lights below. But geographically, everything is wrong. The ocean's a little closer. The neighborhood's a little nicer. There are a couple of broad greenbelts nearby. I'm sure one of them is the LA Country Club's golf course.

The bedroom I'm in is no less breathtaking. Though the color palette is all California mission tones, brown and sand and gold, there's nothing traditional about the furniture. Everything is elegant but practically space-age, looking crafted especially for its place in the room. I've never been in a bed this huge, which seems like a king and a half, with several pillows as long as I am tall. There's a control panel in the nightstand with more buttons than a starship from one of Wade and Fershan's games. Though each of the buttons is accompanied by an icon, I'm hesitant to push anything with novocaine brain still in effect.

"Where the hell..."

I let the query fade. It's not the proper question. Another horse belongs in front of this cart.

*What the hell has happened to me?*

A stab of alarm gives way to crazy flashes of memory.

Reece, waving from the elevator. Adoration in his eyes. My sweatshirt around his waist...

Blasted into nothing by Angelique La Salle. Her siren's smirk. Those cufflinks in her hand...

Blasted apart again, the only choice my heart would allow. Running. Refusing to confront my own stupidity. My blind trust in an idiot's fairy tale...

*Really* blasted then, by the creeps in the train station. Their hands on my body. Their knife in my clothes. Their threats in my ear...

Then the biggest explosion of all.

Him.

Flinging them through the air. Pinning them to the wall. Black leather. Grim fury. Effortless power. Supercharged. Supersonic.

A super hero. Saving me.

"Holy shit."

I sit straight up. Tousle the covers with a bunch of swipes and kicks. Maybe I just need to confirm they're real. That *I'm* still real. That being real won't smash away the memories.

Memories? Or a dream?

"Holy *shit*." I whisper it this time. I run a hand over the sheets and the plain white T-shirt into which I've somehow been changed. It fits me like an oversize gunnysack, but it's as soft as these million-count sheets, smells as clean as cedar, and beats the hell out of the *eau de gangbanger* in which my work clothes are likely drenched by now.

But for all that, I'm still left with no clues about who it really belongs to. *What the hell is going on?*

I'm saved from confusing contemplations about that by a harsh vibration from the nightstand. My phone, inside my purse, is easy enough to grab. I smile in gratitude at the caller's picture and eagerly swipe at the screen.

"Neeta."

"Emma!" The punch of her voice makes me lean away for a second. "*Baap re*! You are okay!"

"I...I think so."

"Where are you?" Her demand is pitched with panic. Before I can come up with a decent answer, instinct steering me away from the obvious, she rushes on. "We saw you. On the news. It was everywhere!"

"On the news?" I shake my head, trying to free it from the fuzz.

"What? Why? How?"

"The security camera feed from the Soto metro station." She takes a huge breath. Her tone softens. "You were attacked, Emma. Do you remember?"

"Yeah," I say too quickly. I rub my forehead with the opposite speed. There's so much to process. *Too* much, even before the most daunting thought of them all thunders back into my gray matter. "Yeah. I remember it all."

Tangible stillness. Then her reverent murmur. "Even the last part?"

"Even the last part."

"So...Bolt is real?"

"Yeah."

*And I think I'm in his apartment right now.*

Fortunately, Neeta's occupied with her own high gasp. "By all the gods. *Emma.*"

I wince. Her fervor slams me, too huge to take in. I'm motion sick, and the only thing turning is the earth on its axis. Maybe if I beg hard enough, God will do me a solid and halt it for a few minutes. "Can... Can I call you back in a little while?" The Almighty will likely want my full attention on the stop-the-globe request.

"Of course. *Wait.*" There's shuffling from her end. Her breaths are hollow, as if she's cupped a hand over her phone. "Are you still with him now?"

"No." Not a lie in the least. I still have no idea what this place is or how I got here. Hell, I don't know if I'm a guest or a hostage—though when I hear a door open somewhere nearby, I sense that answer is near. With heartbeats attacking my throat, I mutter, "Call you back soon," and disconnect the line.

I scramble out of the bed, following the noise despite my uneasiness. Gingerly, I walk toward the sounds.

"Whoa."

I definitely didn't expect...*this*.

First, there's a built-to-fit architectural island constructed out of custom-hewn rocks and curved insets of dark wood. It houses crescent-shaped bookshelves that arch over a curved, see-through fireplace. On either side of the fireplace, narrow steps lead to a sunken reading area with plush couches. A second bookshelf brackets the other side of the area, but instead of a fireplace there's a spirits cabinet.

In short, my idea of heaven on earth.

Sealing the deal? My own angel comes with the package.

He stands in the doorway off to my left, leading to what looks like a bathroom as oversized as the bed. Steam billows around the lean muscles of his towel-wrapped hips, as if he's really just emerged from heaven and the clouds don't want to let go. Can they be blamed? He's glorious, from the bold cut of his abdominal V to the rippled plateaus of his proud shoulders.

And every damp, defined striation in between...

No. *No.*

I don't want this. I don't want him. I *can't* want him.

Because he's not my angel.

Because somehow, in some strange twist of fate, I've ended up here with him—wherever *here* is—and now must deal with looking at him like this. Knowing the shirt he pulled off to *get* like this had cufflinks with it. *Those* cufflinks...

*We were caught up in a...discussion...*

"You're awake," Reece states.

I push one foot back. Another. "Yeah." Finally, I'm able to step away from him. "In a lot more ways than one."

"Velvet—"

"Do. Not." The point is worth halting for. I stand my ground, my gaze on fire from the inside out, one finger stabbing at him. "You don't get to 'velvet' me anymore. Or 'bunny' or 'foo foo' or whatever the hell else you've cooked into that Kool-Aid." I let the finger fall. "I'm not drinking it anymore, Mr. Richards."

"I'm not asking you to drink." He should be given points for not budging from the doorway. "I should have never even asked you to take a sip."

I pivot from him. I know I should let him have that as the last word, accepting accountability for layering more meaning on our fling than he ever should have, but my legs are locked in place. My heart is intractable, clinging to its need for logic. So stupid. There's no logic here. Not with a player like him, who enjoys the big boys' version of chess. Shifting real-life people as his pieces. Playing with their hearts.

No. Not my heart. *You don't get that part, damn it.* "Is that why you had him bring me here?" I peer around again. I don't want to—resisting the interior-design lusties all over again—but I can't help it. "And where *is* here?"

A humorless chuff. "You think I live at the Brocade twenty-four seven?"

I don't answer. Of course that's what I think, especially now. In the space at the hotel, it's simple to slot him into one role. Arrogant, breath-robbing boss man. Here, he's more reachable. More real. He does stuff like read, sleep...take showers.

"And who, exactly, did I have bring you here?"

"You know who." I stab him with a glare as vicious as my tone. "That...person. Or whatever he is. Bolt. You know him somehow, don't you? So you contacted him after I passed out. Or maybe you had him knock me out somehow..." Which is a disturbing thought, so I don't finish it.

"Why would you think I know him?"

I ignore the subtle scalpel in his tone too. I don't want to be nicked by whatever has sharpened it. Apprehension? Tension? Do I care?

I shouldn't. I can't.

"Don't you know *all* the special people, Mr. Richards?" I finish it off with pure snark before descending the stairs to the sunken reading heaven. I shouldn't be doing this, purposely closing the gap to such incredible temptation, but I refuse to keep talking to him anywhere near the bed. "People like Angelique La Salle?"

Perfect words for reinforcing my resolve. The man may be only wearing a towel now, but less than twenty-four hours ago he was in the backseat of that woman's car—letting her take off his cufflinks. And the logical things that came after that.

Reece doesn't follow me down the stairs. He remains on the higher level, arms folded, feet braced, once more in misplaced pharaoh mode. If the towel were tucked differently and he had one of those fancy gold pharaoh turbans, then yeah. But that would mean covering his hair...

"You think Angelique La Salle is 'special' to me?"

I fold my arms too and push out a confused huff. The question isn't rhetorical, but it sure as hell isn't compassionate. He wants—demands—an answer.

"You going to tell me she's not?"

He hauls in a long breath. While letting it out, he steps down to my level, though little else changes. He's still in his Ruler of the Nile stance. His gaze is the color of armor in the rain.

"She used to be…a good friend," he finally murmurs. "She was in town. I met her so I could return some things to her."

"Like a pair of cufflinks?"

His next inhalation is sharper. "Yes. Among other things."

I glower carefully. "Good friends." I tell myself not to finish it… but what other choice is there? Bleed out slowly or just rip the damn bandage off? "How good?"

"We were…involved. About a year and a half ago."

I back up by a step. Swallow hard. It's the blood I asked for, just not the pain I expected. "Involved." And as long as I'm hemorrhaging… "Like lovers?"

His posture tightens. The sight of it is both exquisite and excruciating. The man isn't built like a tank, but the creator spared no detail on his lean, beautiful body. His muscles are carefully carved, utterly decadent.

"No," he states at last. "Not like lovers."

"So you didn't fuck her?"

"Oh, I fucked her a lot. But she was *not* my lover." He drills his gaze into me, intense as lightning. "She let you believe something differently, didn't she? When she came to the hotel. When she tried to bring back those goddamned cufflinks."

"But how did..." I shake my head, answering my own question. "The security cams. The same way you knew I'd left the hotel, right?"

"Yeah." He draws out the word, making room for a strange subtext in his tone. I'd usually call it tension, but not the same kind I've seen in him before. This stress is different. It doesn't make him scary anymore. It makes him vulnerable. "Something like that."

"Something like that." Damn it, I want to ignore that tenderness—to pretend that side of him isn't speaking out at the wrong, wrong, *wrong* damn time—but I can't. "How?"

His composure tightens. "What did Angelique say to you?" he counters. "You two talked. She was at the desk for a while."

I turn from him again, for a couple of different reasons. One, it's hard to remember my own name with him in that towel, let alone what his bombshell of an ex dropped on me in the conversation last night. I go ahead and voice number two out loud. "Why should I answer your question when you won't acknowledge mine?"

"Because your answer is going to help me keep you safe."

"Safe?" I practically laugh out the word. If I don't laugh, I'll cry—and hell if I'll let him see *that*. "That's a funny term to me right now, buddy."

"I am aware of that, Emma."

"Are you?" *Now* it's time to get delirious. And pissed. And outraged. And scared. I think "scared" might be the newest word in my permanent vocabulary. "Are you really *aware*, Mr. Richards, of my 'safety' when it comes to your crafty ex?"

His hands coil. His jaw squares. He jerks his head, raining drops from his hair over the taut slabs of his chest and the chiseled dessert tray of his abs—but dessert isn't an option as he slowly steps closer, brandishing hard eyes and flaring nostrils.

"Crafty?" He growls the word but punctuates with a harsh chuff. "Crafty. Well, there's a piece of funny."

"Excuse the hell out of me?"

He breathes in through his nostrils and exhales with vicious force. "I think you don't know *shit* about 'crafty,' Emmalina—and that scares me most of all." He leans over, skewing the towel sideways, exposing the strain of his extended hip—not that I get more than a glance as his ire blatantly grows. "'Crafty' is a word for your shoe-eating dog, your scrapbooking neighbor, or the grandma who makes Christmas wreaths out of used soda cans. It's *not* the word for my lunatic bitch of an ex-girlfriend." He closes the gap between us and opens one of those fists to grab my shoulder. "Do I make myself fucking clear?"

My breath wads at the back of my throat, congeals, and turns into a boulder before crashing into my gut. Forget considering his vulnerable side. What he reveals now isn't even a run-of-the-mill soft side. This is him, genuinely spooked by the idea of Angelique even talking to me last night.

Angelique. His "lunatic bitch of an ex."

A claim that should mean something—more than what it means now. But every time it seems like the man rips a mask off for me, another is swept into its place and glued firmly on. I know he's telling me the truth—just not all of it.

Not the biggest part of it.

"Reece? What the hell?" I let him hear every note of my desperate confusion. Let him feel the force of my searching stare. But if I make a dent in his ire, it's impossible to tell. His features remain the texture of solid, inscrutable granite.

"I *said*," he finally growls, "do I make myself *clear*?"

I huff out a sigh. "Yes." I wrench my arm away—or try to. "Now let me go." When he's as responsive as a ninja gripping a katana, I resort to yelling. "*Reece.*"

When he jerks his stare up, his eyes are glazed.

"Let me go or tell me what the hell is going on. Do I make *that* fucking clear?"

## REECE

My hand slips from her shoulder.

*Let me go...*

A breath slowly flows from her body.

*Or tell me what the hell is going on...*

With equal sadness, she takes a step back. Then another.

Only in that moment, in the dip of her head and the stiffness of her shoulders, am I bulldozed by an awful recognition.

Warning her away from Angelique, I've done nothing to protect her—and everything to alienate her.

She's just as fucking serious as I've been. Letting her go...means *letting her go.*

No. *No,* damn it. Not an option.

Which means I have to consider unveiling what's behind door number two.

"Emmalina."

She stops, one foot angled on the corner of a stair. She waits, hands at her sides with fingernails jabbing into her palms. I watch her wrists shake from the effort—knowing I'm the cause of her pain.

Hating myself for it.

*Goddamnit.*

Hating myself for every dumbass, douchebag move I've ever pulled, from sticking my dick in the crazy of Angelique to landing myself right here, right now—wondering how the hell I'm going to break this to the most amazing woman I've ever met.

There's no instruction manual for this.

Isn't there supposed to be *be* an instruction manual somewhere? *Congratulations! You're a super hero! Quick and easy FAQs, including how to talk to your doctor, your dry cleaner, and your girlfriend.*

And during my dumbass sulk, she's moved on, turned away, and cleared the stairs.

*"Emmalina."*

This time, she doesn't stop. She leans over the bed to scoop up her phone, derailing every damn thought in my mind again with a peek of her ass, perfectly cupped by her pale-pink panties...

*Christ.* There needs to be a chapter in the manual about dealing with panties too.

"Please. *Shit.* Emma. Damn it!"

She stops and straightens but doesn't turn back. "Reece... I..." The nightstand light throws golden light across the side of her face and the cloud of her hair, transforming her into a vision of innocence and illicitness in one breath-stealing second. "Look, I want to..." She sets down her phone and pushes out a soft *tsk*, as if admonishing *herself* for this tension between us. "I just want to say thank you, all right? Whatever this is, or *was*, between us...it was really awesome, but—"

"Goddamnit." I stomp up the stairs. "No way. We're not a 'was.' We're *not—*"

"Reece." She grabs one of my hands with both of hers and lifts a wistful smile. "We're not even a 'we,' and that's okay. It's not good or bad or wrong or right. It just *is*. You have a lot going on. I mean, you're...*you*...and—"

"Fuck." I yank my hand back and drag it through my hair. Punch out a wry laugh. "No, Emma. I'm not me. I mean, I'm not him. That guy you think I am. That prick—"

"You're not a prick."

"Not anymore."

"Not ever." She pushes forward, lifting her hands to bracket my jaw. Her immense gaze pulls me in, the aqua light mesmerizing every neuron in my body. "It took you a little while to free the good man hiding underneath that other one, but he's there. *I* see him, I believe in him, and he's beautiful. Now you just have to believe too."

My snarl is guttural and deep—and angry. I jerk my head in vicious defiance, setting my face into a *don't-cross-me* expression. "You have *no* damn idea what you're talking about."

The woman actually hurls back her own growl. The defiance is so breathtaking, I'm reduced to a stunned stare as she pushes on. "Oh yeah? Who came down from the spire, rolled up his sleeves, and helped us turn the rooms for the tour group during that crunch?"

"And snagged a nice fringe benefit from the deal?" I jab a knowing smirk.

"Okay, then. Who's the guy who keeps insisting on paying Zalkon every day just to haul my backside to and from work?"

"You mean when you'll keep your backside *at* work?"

"I think my backside gets an excuse note after last night."

"I think it deserves a number of notes on *any* night."

She whacks my shoulders. "You're ignoring the point."

"Which was what again?" Not that I've forgotten. More like I hope *she's* forgotten—since I'm beginning to. *Fast.* Discussing any part of this woman's anatomy, much less the hot temptation of her backside, derails my senses, consumes my will, blazes every drop of my blood. For the first time in my life, I really know the meaning of *obsession*—in the best and worst ways.

"That I'm not going to let you get away with the 'just a dick' excuse?" Despite her sassy tone, her hands haven't moved off my shoulders. I watch them now, as she starts exploring my collarbones with her fingertips. It feels so fucking good. I clench back a savoring moan.

*Just a dick. Oh, Velvet. If you knew exactly how much I could validate that...*

To turn her explorations into my seduction. To chisel her point down to craving *my* point. To make her forget everything except the one thing I *can* do better than anyone else.

Which will do what?

Delay the inevitable, *that's* what.

*Tell her—or let her go.*

"You're still not convinced, are you?"

Her prod makes me chuckle. "That I'm a dick?"

"Ugggghhh." She bats at me again. Though I attempt another laugh, she refuses to join in. "Fine. As long as we're talking about my lame move from last night, who was the 'dick' who tracked me down to the train station and then came and got me—after I passed out in another guy's arms?"

I almost laugh again. It's the way I roll when fate opens a door so hard, the wood knocks me between the eyes. But I'm not spinning so hard that I don't see the gaping break she's handed over.

It's time to jump through.

No matter how black the abyss on the other side.

"Yeah...uh...about that 'other guy'..."

## EMMA

Weird.

It was the word Neeta, Wade, and Fershan whispered that first night I'd met Reece. The word I'd been irked about, much less couldn't understand. The word that's lingered at the back of my mind this whole week, mostly because it still hasn't made any damn sense when it comes to him...

Until now.

*Now,* he's weird. Not even that. His vibe is something I just don't get. Enigmatic? Cryptic?

Scary?

The descriptor fits better than the others, but I don't want it to. But something about how he takes both my hands and guides me to sit on the bed sears my spine with nothing *but* scared. The apprehension worsens when he releases me to take a measured step back. He breathes in, as if preparing to peel back his lips and reveal gleaming fangs.

I sit up straighter. "Okaaayyy," I finally utter. "Reece? What is it?" I manage to grab one of his hands again, tightening my hold around his stiff fingers. "That other guy? What are you..." A frown sets in. "You mean Bolt?" Another slice of fear, though he reaches for the nightstand drawer as if he's just searching for a tissue. "What happened with him? Shit. What did he do?" I shove furious air through my nostrils. "Did he hurt *you*? Because, I swear to God, if he tried to—"

I freeze as he turns, trailing something from the drawer between two of his long fingers.

Not a tissue. A mask.

A sleek, black, Maserati mask.

"What...the..."

He lets the molded leather fall to my lap. I look at it like he's dropped a killer spider.

"I...don't understand. Where did you—" My breaths come faster and faster. "Did he give this to you? Like a souvenir?"

He laughs. Not hard, but enough to make me want to smack him again. No. Punch him. He needs to be telling me I'm right—that the leather in my lap is just a gift from his buddy or a memento found on the train platform.

Because if I'm not right, that means...

*Oh shit, oh shit, oh shit.*

"He didn't give me the mask, Emmalina."

...that every knowing note in his tone is right...

"Then why was it in your nightstand?"

...that every ounce of dread in mine is too...

"Because it's mine."

...that the unreal is suddenly very real.

I lurch to my feet and force them to move in a frantic figure eight, countering my exploding mind and churning stomach. My fist twists against the molded leather game-changer he's just laid on me. My other hand opens and closes in time to my wild-woman pace.

"But not because it's *yours* yours, right?"

When he issues nothing but silence, I freeze in place, gaping at him with new urgency. Mentally, I drop the towel from his body and redress him in black leather. My imagination secures the mask across the chiseled planes of his face.

All too easily, the result blooms in my mind. All too clearly, I can see him in that god-in-leather finery. Filling it with his regal posture. Turning it into visual poetry with his stride, his grace.

Dominating the very air he's in.

Controlling it. Using it.

Like his weapon.

*The guy's weird, Emma.*

*He's not the person you think, Emma.*

"Shit." I sink back to the bed. "*Shit.*"

"Emma—"

"It *is* yours." I lift my head, staring, as if seeing him for the first time. "Because you're...him."

He averts his gaze. Twists his lips into a ruthless grimace. "I'm just me, Emma. And I'm just trying, for the first time, to do something with my life besides being paparazzi food. What everyone else chooses to call it, or how they want to glorify it..." He shrugs, turning the errant drops on his shoulders into planes of muscled luster. "That's not up to me."

After letting that statement steep in a long silence, I murmur, "Which is why you've kept it a secret."

"Among other reasons, yes."

"But you finally did tell me."

I lift the mask, still dangling from my palm, back toward him.

I'm not sure what I'm trying to tell him with the act, but he gazes at the leather with the same intensity I do, knowing the gesture stands for something. Not my total understanding—that may not ever come—but perhaps my gratitude. Exposing himself like this... It's taken trust that turns his body into a block of tension and his energy into a strained matrix.

He accepts the mask from me and drops the leather piece back on the nightstand. He sits down next to me, curling one of his hands with mine. "Because it was tell you or lose you."

I turn, taking in his face more intently. Most specifically, the truth now speaking to me from his eyes. "But you're still not sure I won't run away flailing."

I don't expect his sardonic snort. "I'm just a guy playing the odds, beauty."

I turn my hand in, twining my fingers with his. Comprehension slams hard. The recognition that, despite the informational warhead he dropped a minute ago, *this* moment blows me away more. The rogue savior of our city, the idol who's fascinated the land of the jaded, is sitting next to me wrapped in nothing but a towel and a lot of uncertainty. A super hero who keeps his mask in the nightstand has clearly placed his heart in my hands.

Is this really my life?

Am I really lifting his hand and gently turning it over to trace a finger along the pulse beneath his wrist? Am I really watching a tremor take him, rolling through him like a bank of summer thunder, turning his blood vessels into a web of lightning? Are his fingers actually glowing blue and gold against mine, their light corresponding to the heavy breaths pumping his sculpted chest?

"Tell me." My whisper is weighted by demand as much as curiosity. I join a second finger to my first, flowing my touch up his arm...watching the amazing light of his bloodstream beneath his skin.

Beneath my touch, Reece's limbs jerk and shudder. He grips me, digging into my hips, all but pleading with me to keep exploring him like that. "Tell you what?" he grates. "You can have anything, Velvet. *Everything.*"

I lean in and lift a hand to the thick artery pumping down the side of his neck. I watch it light up like a hose holding radioactive acid. I stroke a little harder. The glint intensifies. "Is this why you always ordered me to close my eyes?"

He swallows deeply. "Yeah."

I lift my head, confronting the gorgeous glow from his pupils too. "It's beautiful."

"*You're* beautiful." He pulls my fingers to his lips. His kiss carries a tiny shock, inciting a gasp. He does it again, sending a similar zap to the tender tissues between my legs.

I angle my body more toward his. He releases my fingers and settles his incredible lips over mine. I thread my touch through his hair as we kiss for long tender moments. Static flows in the wake of my fingers, transferring white-hot energy back into my hand and up my arm.

"Wow." I let out a delighted laugh.

"No shit." His commiserating grin is mesmerizing.

"Dork." I say it as a tease but turn sober enough to add, "As if all this is new for *you*?"

He kisses me again. New energy arcs between us, making us

both gasp and quiver. "Every moment."

"Bullshit."

"*No* shit." He dares me to doubt him with a harder, deeper kiss. Well over a minute later, when he lets me up for air once more, I openly gawk.

"So...you *weren't* kidding the other night? About it being a while?" I watch the slow, steady shake of his head. "Because of... what happened to make you this way?" Refusing to accept his thick silence as an answer, I tug at his hair. As silken as the strands are, I stay focused. "You said I could ask anything, Reece. That you'd give it to me."

His brow furrows. I can all but hear him cursing himself, but that won't get him a bye on my purpose. *I need to know.*

"This shit...it's part of me now," he finally utters. "It's in my blood, my sweat, my nervous system..."

"And you didn't know what that would do to someone if you were intimate with them."

I release a long breath as the understanding sinks in. He answers by jerking another nod.

"To be honest, my head wasn't even there anyway. My life was ass-backward and upside down, and all I cared about was righting it again."

"Then why did you end up here?"

"In LA?"

"Yeah."

"I don't understand."

"Richards Resorts International is headquartered in New York. You're as far away from that as the contiguous states will allow."

"And?"

"Well, if you're trying to get your shit together, why did your dad banish you out here?" I tilt my head. "You have to know that's what everyone is saying, right? That the family sent you out here for some heavy shit that went down in Europe. Parties? Women? Drugs?"

He chuffs. "Yeah. That's all still pretty funny."

I right myself. "So it *didn't* happen like that?"

His stare turns droll. "Hell if *I* know, Velvet."

"You were too strung-out to remember?"

"I was too *not there* to remember."

I blink hard. Then again. "But there were pictures of you..."

"Cut, pasted, and altered, and then strategically released to the media," he supplies.

"*What*?" I gape. "For how long?"

"Nearly six months."

"*Why*?"

"So nobody would figure out where I really was." He cuts me short from the logical follow-up to that with a look I can only describe as shellshock. He juts his jaw, inhaling deep once more. "It was six months of fucking hell, and that's the only 'everything' you get about it."

My heart squeezes. My throat constricts. Air is my new enemy, hurting with every intake, as I slide my hand to the back of his neck. I wrap my other arm around his waist, rejoicing as he pulls me even tighter.

Just like that, it's back—that sizzling, encompassing force field of his, binding our energies like lightning in storm clouds but with a thousand times more magic. I give into it with a jagged sigh, tucking my lips against his neck. I press kisses from his ear to his jaw and back again. His breaths rumble into my hair, sparking more fierce need between us. My pulse sprints to match his. My hand races up and down his spine. I marvel at his corded strength bunching beneath my touch like power cables wrapped in satin. Tanned, taut, muscle-laced satin. I yearn to dissolve into him, to tangle myself with him. The admission pushes another shaky breath through me, echoed by a similar sound in his chest.

Between those rough breaths, I finally compose words. "Wow." Okay, one word. Saying it all, yet saying nothing. How do I tell him he's fried the neurons of my mind? Blown apart every imagining of my soul? Given my heart one of the greatest gifts it could ever receive? How do I tell him *all* that, without making it about Bolt?

Because he'll never believe me. I even wonder if I'll believe myself.

Because without the hell he endured to become this man in my arms, he likely wouldn't *be* the man in my arms.

And I've fallen helplessly, hopelessly in love with the man in my arms.

The man who envelopes me tighter in his hold, wreathing my torso in greater sparks of awareness and awakening, before whispering, "Wow is a damn good start."

"A start." I trail my mouth down to his shoulder. I breathe him in, all fresh sandalwood soap with a hint of his natural smoke and cedar, while sliding my tongue over every fascinating muscle of his shoulder. "But...*just* a start, right?"

"Only if you'll have me for more." He issues it in a soft snarl, which quickly becomes a fierce choke. The sound bites the air as I do the same to the bottom of his neck. "*Fuck,* Emma. Say you'll have me."

He digs a hand deeper into my waist, bunching fingers into my shirt. *His* shirt. I revel in the awareness. I'm in *his* bed, wearing *his* shirt. And now, I'm twisting to straddle his lap before planting my knees in his sheets. I'm surrounded by him—his scent, his fabrics, his bed, his energy—razing me from scalp to soles, inciting one consuming need in return.

To surround *him* with *me.*

"I'll have you, Reece Richards." I brace my thumb and forefinger against his jaw, securing him with possessive intent. "I'll have you. I want you."

*I love you.*

For a second, I'm terrified I've let it escape aloud. The way his whole frame stills—stopping as if I've shot him in the chest—has me dropping my hand. His features take on a new hardness. His gaze beams with a force *nobody* would question twice. A message confirmed by every thrumming, throbbing, cell of my body.

He craves me too.

He shows me exactly that, lunging in until our lips collide. He's untamed shrapnel in my mouth, everywhere at once, setting me afire with every sweep of his tongue. In response, I give a shaky, needy moan. I'm already collateral damage, gutted from his assault, gorging on his passion...

Ripping off his towel.

Looking down at him—all of him—with savoring hunger.

Rejoicing in every magnificent muscle I see. And caress. And spark into electrified glory as his blood heats and pulses and funnels to the most fascinating bolt in his body...

I wrap both hands around his cock and stroke him from glowing balls to the bold beacon of his head, wanting him worse than I ever have before.

# CHAPTER ELEVEN

## REECE

"Emma. *Fuck.*" Both words are barely breaths, breaking past my locked teeth as her talented fingers coax more heat to the surface of my cock. *Surface?* Who am I kidding? Every inch of me, from the core of throbbing magma to the veins pounding at my stretched skin, is a new slave to her mastery, a new convert to her religion.

And what does my new goddess give me in return? A stare brimming with just as much adoration, worship, amazement, devotion. Blowing me away. Spinning my senses. That's before she even speaks again.

"Reece. It's beautiful." She drops her head, brushing the glowing drop off my tip with her lips. "*You're* so beautiful."

I smile. At least I think I do. It's hard to know what's real right now. "You mean that, don't you?" My astonishment is authentic. "You don't think I'm a freak? That this is fifteen kinds of weird?"

"Of course it's weird." She licks her lips, spreading the sheen of my pre-come across their delectable curves like space-age lip gloss. "But it's wonderful. And incredible."

"And freaky?"

"Oh, that's the best part."

I join my gruff laugh to her sighing giggle as she resumes touching me. Squeezing me. Gazing at me. Fuck, yes. That's the best part. Getting to see her eyes, wide as Caribbean seas, drenching my body with their heat and light and lust. Seeing that even though I could lead Santa's fucking sleigh with my cock, she still can't stop touching it and then kissing it once more.

"*Fuck.*" My hips convulse as she sucks off more drops from my strained head. "Velvet...baby...that's..."

"Freaky." She laughs it out while kissing her way up my torso. Her lips, still heated by the drops she just took in, close over one of my nipples. "Guess it's a good thing I'm into freaks." Then the other.

"*Damn* good thing." I cup the back of her neck, directing her to do it again. She flattens her tongue, forming a hot wet trail between my pecs, as I use my other hand to push at the T-shirt covering her. Though she's turned white cotton into a fashion statement I'll never tire of, naked is how I need her right now. Her tits are what I crave, smashed against my chest, smeared in the same fiery river blazing the plain over my heart.

I finally strip the shirt away from her. With a starving growl, I yank her down to me. In a crazy torrent, we kiss. Bite. Devour. Spar. Fighting to expel our passion while feeding the damn monster with every passing second. It's frenzied, fiery, passionate, and frightening, and I never want it to be any other way.

Hell. It was the word I just used to tell her what made me this way.

A hell I'll endure again, a thousand times over, if she's the prize waiting at the end.

"Oh my...*wow!*" she exclaims against my lips as her breasts crush my chest. I lift a smile in return, nipping at the soft nectar of her mouth.

"One way of putting it." I scrape her chin with my teeth before jerking at her hair, compelling her head back. The exposed column of her neck is creamy and smooth...and ready for my mark. Needing to be branded.

I lift my head, growling as she gasps, scoring her skin with my rough kiss. Between our bodies, my cock jerks and grows. More arousal spurts from my head, soaking the cotton barrier of her panties. I curl my head tighter to look down there. The sight of the spot I've made, turning the satin from light pink to dark, unhinges something even more feral in me. Something that needs that underwear out of my way. *Now.*

I twist a couple of fingers into the sweet pink lace and jerk hard—only to have the material battle my grip. *Damn it.*

I lift her and flip her all the way over. Pushing back for leverage, I'm treated to the world's best aerial view. The landscape of her body is a silken dream, topped by the succulent berries of her erect nipples. All I need to see now is the bare peach between her thighs.

A satisfaction I need this second.

"Close your eyes, Emma. Only for a second, beauty," I add as she sends an are-you-serious glower. I make good on the promise, pulling up on the lace at her hip so it's nearly a taut pink rope—and now, a perfect target for the blue laser my forefinger becomes.

Inside a second, I sear the material away. Emma's gaze pops open as the smoking satin falls from her body. I take a deep breath, forcing the heat to subside, though it's damn awesome not to worry about hiding my ten lightsabers anymore.

*Very* awesome.

"Holy...wow."

I wiggle my fingers slowly...before lowering their tips to the graceful ridges of her pubic bones. "Wow," I echo, spreading my touch outward, coaxing her thighs to spread the same direction. "You enjoy that word, don't you?"

"In this case, it fits." As my thumbs meet, toying with the top of her pouting slit, her hips writhe. "It fits *you*."

I work my thumbs downward and spread the rest of my fingers along her pulsing lips, reveling in how they eagerly kiss at the air. "Fitting *you* is my goal, Miss Crist."

"Oh," she mewls. The sound deepens and darkens as I work my thumbs in more, spreading her wet depths. Soon, I'm pushing into her as well, a tender but steady finger fuck. My other fingers spread out, keeping her thighs apart. I brace my elbows against her knees— which start to shake, becoming erotic turn-ons in their own right. Holy hell. Because of her, I'm now a knee guy.

Fuck.

Because of her, I'm now an everything guy.

"Reece."

"Emma."

"*Reece!*"

I replace my fingertips with my hips and gulp hard at how good her inner thighs feel against me. At how good *all* of her feels against me.

"Open wider for me, beauty." I lean over, kissing her in long, passionate pulls as she complies. "Yeah. Like that." My own breath stutters. "Do you know how many times I've imagined being with you like this? Completely bare like this?" I skate my touch back up over her puckered breasts. Watching her nipples light up beneath my touch is a turn-on beyond the dreams I've just referenced. "No holding anything back. No more hiding."

Emma clutches my hand and guides it to the side of her face. "Never again." Her tawny lashes lift. Her stare is pure blue conviction, engulfing mine. "No more hiding."

I curve my fingers in, catching the edge of her hairline, outlining her features with an ethereal glow. *My* glow. "Fuck." I gulp hard, struggling to put what I feel into words, but finally accept that uselessness. I can only stare, gutted and grateful, for what she's done for me in this moment. Her elegant profile illuminated like this turns my garishness into a gift, my curse into inspiration.

Because of her, I'm no longer a victim. I'm a survivor.

I'm stronger.

And maybe, someday, I can even think of calling myself a hero.

For right now, it only matters that she sees me as one.

With her eyes glimmering and her lips parted, she releases my hand and slides her touch up my arm. Once she gets to my shoulder, she doesn't stop. Tremors radiate across my back as she skates her hand down, skimming past my waist, before molding a palm across my ass. Before I can process how fucking good *that* feels, she grips my other cheek too.

Pulling me closer to her softness. Urging me deeper into her beauty.

I fall onto my elbows. Our faces are inches apart. Her eyes are like sapphire smoke. Her skin is a sheen of arousal. I inhale as she exhales. Her breath smells like sex... The essence she's already kissed off my cock. The desire I have yet to sate.

The lust with which she claws into my ass, seating me tighter between her legs.

"Light me up, Reece." Her voice is a shimmering, demanding plea. "*Do it.* Light me up. From the inside."

"Emma." I shake now too, fighting to restrain myself. There are more words to be said here. Words that must be said. Shit about being careful and grabbing condoms and...

"It's all right." She rocks beneath me, lithe and lusty, taunting my dick with the soft, soaked layers of her pussy. "I'm on the pill. I didn't tell you before, because—" She interrupts herself, coloring a little. "Well, because..."

I kiss her nose in reassurance. "It's all right, beauty. I get it."

"And now you've got *me*." She lifts her legs, crossing them at the small of my back. "And I need *you*. Please. All of you. Every freaky, weird, magnificent, glowing inch of—*oh*!"

As hot as I am, she's hotter.

As taut as I am, she's tighter.

As bright as I am, she's so much brighter. Illuminated. Ablaze. A sensual, incredible angel, looking like a goddamned page out of a comic book herself. Her hair fans against my sheets as if she's flying. Her face, surrounded by my neon fingers, is alight with strength, sensuality, surrender, joy. Her body, spread for me, is a collection of muscle and might and power—especially in the center of the gem where we're joined. As we rock, completely in sync with each other, the light of that juncture pulses and intensifies.

"Ohhhh!" She screams it again as I shove at her legs.

"Ohhhh!" Once more as I stretch her deeper.

"Ohhhh!" Even louder as I slam into the tight, dripping oval welcoming my cock.

I stop only for a second to grab at the pillows and bunch them behind her head. "No more closed eyes, Emmalina." I angle her head down, ensuring she focuses toward the sight of her body sucking me in, over and over and over. "Watch," I dictate. "*Watch me.*"

"Yes." Her breath-filled obedience is like rocket fuel to every inch of my dick. "*Yes.*"

My balls constrict.

The fusion of our bodies is raw radiance.

"Do you like the freak fucking you?"

The beast inside me growls into my words, feeling so damn good to be let out.

"Don't see any freaks around here, Mr. Richards." She puts a coy spin on the smirk. "You sure you got the right address for that claim?"

"Oh, I'm sure."

"Better check again." Her eyelids go heavy, emphasizing the tease of her pouting lips. "Or...knock a little harder."

My grin splits wider.

My cock swells against her walls.

"You are *really* asking for it, Miss Crist."

"Damn right I am, freak."

I'm not sure what drives me more blissfully insane—the sexy sarcasm in her tease or the come-on in her eyes. In the end, it doesn't matter. In the end, I'm ramming her tight, perfect cunt with all the force I can flex into my hips, all the power I can surge into my cock...

all the passion I can summon to my spirit.

All the pleasure, heat, and fire I can give her—bursting into the high, aching joy of her climax.

"Reece!"

*"Emma."*

"Need...you...with me!"

"On my way, beauty."

Not a lie.

Because I am. Because I do.

My cock isn't just the color of a laser beam anymore. It feels like a laser beam, consumed by a cataclysm and pushing through the cosmos of blinding heat and fury until it bursts like a goddamn star, pouring liquid life into ultimate darkness. Fucking and fucking and fucking, until there's nothing left of the light anymore.

But everything left of the ashes. And the freak is rising from them like the most bizarre new phoenix in the history of ashes. A guy I'm not sure I recognize. A man who might actually be ready for this super hero gig.

Like he just might have something worthy to add to the narrative.

Not that I'm ready to go spreading that shit around.

I mean, it's just a thought. At the end of the day, I'm a man more used to VIP ropes than police tape. I'm happier finding discrepancies on spreadsheets than tracking down bad guys in sewers. I thought it might be the right thing to do, after all the douchebag moments to which I've subjected the world, to pay back Karma—and, yeah, The Consortium—by going out in a blaze of glory instead of headlines of scandal. Who thought a few do-the-right-thing moments might actually *feel* right too.

Not that I was ever really taught anything about "right." In boarding school, "conduct" and "character" were ideologies to make fun of between chasing tail and sneaking booze, not part of the life lessons I ever learned from Chase Richards.

Maybe that's why I question how good everything feels now. *How right.*

It's her. Emmalina. I'm obsessed with her beauty, slammed by her passion, floored by her purpose, consumed by her simple but sublime wonder. And I know, even if the world never does, that with this, with her, I got shit right at least once in my life.

I know it with the certainty still flooding me, hours later, when I drag my eyes open and still find her in my bed. I know it as I reach over to brush hair from her face and feel a smile breach my lips in tandem with the one curling hers. I know it with every thump of the heartbeat rising to greet her touch as she slides over and burrows against me.

"Mmm." She inflects it with kittenish gusto. "You're warm."

"And you don't even have to plug me in."

"Oh, there's another one for the he's-a-keeper column." Her teeth snag her bottom lip. "*Not* that you're a *keeper* keeper. I mean, not like that. I mean"—she gulps—"*shit*. Can I have a do over?"

"Not on your fucking life." I jam a firm kiss to her forehead. "I like being your keeper." I slide my lips down the bridge of her nose. "Just say you'll be mine too."

"I want to. But Reece..."

"Yeah?" *Stay open. Stay calm.* But that's easier said than done. I'm the one used to doling out this kind of anxiety. Suffering it is *no* fucking fun.

She flattens a hand over my sternum again and gazes right into my eyes. "I need to know everything." A careful swallow. "About Angelique."

I roll to my back and suck in a long breath. She shifts too, rolling to lie on her side next to me. "What about her?"

"She's the one, isn't she?" Her query is soft and knowing. "The one you trusted. Who led you into the hell that changed everything."

I snort out a laugh. She looks like I just hurled in the bed. Not sure I don't want to, especially when replying. "I wasn't exactly white milk, apple pie, and innocence about the whole thing, okay? I met the woman in Paris, in a club where condoms and blow were offered on the menu next to appetizers, and the private rooms were more crowded than the dance floor. We did the circuit there together for a week, and I was enthralled because she knew more people than I did."

I'm not comfortable, but I keep going. She deserves the truth, and in this case, the truth doesn't come in a scrapbook surrounded by hearts and flowers.

"When she told me the scene in Barcelona was more interesting than Paris, I jumped at the chance to follow her there. She played me perfectly, knowing the exact bait to dangle. I wanted the goodies none of my friends had seen yet. The experience none of them could buy through the normal channels."

Emma curls her hand into a fist, forms her other hand over it, and then parks her chin on the stack. "You wanted more."

Three simple words, meaning so much. Meaning too much.

"Maybe." It's more like *probably,* but it feels wrong to lay the filter of my depraved life over the earnest honesty of hers. To her, "more" has been a synonym for expanding her world. To the man I was, it was a chance to get off on new thrills and expand my empire of illicitness.

Pathetic, stupid man. Grasping small, insignificant dreams.

I had the capacity to do so much more. To be so much more.

Thank fuck she's there again, her tender voice hauling me out of my moroseness. "So what happened then?"

"We'd been in Barcelona a few nights. I was getting bored with the scene, but Angelique kept me on her string—and finally told me about a private rave on the outskirts of the city. A real Bohemian bash in some secret warehouse with designer drugs and royal family cousins and shit."

She contemplates that with a tight look. "Only it wasn't a party."

At first, I give her only thick silence. I use the pause to turn my stare back up at the ceiling. I reach to the back of her head and comb my fingers through her strands, using the movement as subliminal Zen. "You know that urban legend about the businessman who sleeps with the hooker, gets drugged, and wakes up missing a kidney? It was sort of like that, but if there was sex first I missed it, and the 'hooker' was a bunch of big guys in lab coats telling me they'd formed a global conglomeration called The Consortium."

"The *what*?" She stiffens. "What the hell does that even mean?"

"Wasn't sure. And I didn't care, since I'd just been checked into a joint that sure as hell wasn't the Ritz. Slowly but surely, they let me in on the joke—but it wasn't a joke. I'd been recruited as a subject in their groundbreaking research in the field of human DNA improvement through electronic enhancement."

She jerks upright and stares as if I'm about to reveal the big joke of the story, but with her lungs pumping frantically, she knows I'm not. She hears my truth. And crazily, *crucially*, she believes it. "Oh, my God," she rasps.

I shrug again. It looks caustic, but I know she sees that truth too—that it's the sarcastic shield to lessen the stain of the memories. "God wasn't around much," I mutter. "Plenty of his son-of-a-bitch friends, though. What's that fun expression? Devil's in the details?"

With that, even fixating on the ceiling won't help. I push away the covers, roll to the side of the bed, and plant my feet on the floor to make the room stop spinning—and keep the cockroaches of memory from invading my mind. "Those bastards were *very* detailed."

I let my eyes slide shut. In my mind, I escape to visions of mountains and meadows and peace... My refuge when the lab and the walls and the pain threatened to drown out everything I was.

Not working. Not anymore.

What works now...is her.

Emma's fingers, soft as wind, brushing my hunched shoulders. Her body, like a waterfall, draping across my back. Her kisses, healing as herbs, following my jawline. She coaxes me back, willing my body back, though my mind clings to the fear. The vow I made to myself over and over again during those months before one of the guards got careless with my shackles one night, giving me the sole chance to escape that hell.

But along with that memory, I also recall the mantra. The vow I swore I'd never forget—or betray.

*Never. Trust. Again.*

A year. I've honored the crap out of every syllable of that oath through every second of every day for the last goddamned year.

Haven't even been tempted to abandon it.

Until now.

Until, bathing in the perfection of her touch and the light of her comfort, I'm torn to let it all go. To let her all the way in. I've already given her the truth of my existence, and she's already returned it with the gifts of her adoration, her acceptance, her passion. But there's more. So much more. So much still bricked-up and blocked—those parts of me that were young and arrogant and stupid. Maybe they don't even exist anymore. *I* haven't even looked behind the wall in a year. Maybe they were fried by the lightning and are now shriveled husks in the heart that once pledged to keep them alive, hoping some extraordinary someone would come along to heal them one day.

Someone like her.

"You're not there anymore, Reece. You're right here, and you're perfectly safe with me."

"Thanks." I want to add more but can't. The vow has been embedded deep into my psyche.

*Never. Trust. Again.*

"Hey." Her fresh tone, inching toward a little playfulness, makes my head perk up. "You got any wheels around here? Other than Z's?"

I bark in laughter. Before she can deliver much of a confused scowl, I sweep off the bed, scoop up the T-shirt, and toss it at her. I fish into the dresser for a pair of my drawstring shorts, usually reserved for home gym workouts, and add the Pentatonix sweatshirt I borrowed from her last night. "Those'll fit you for now. Come on."

A few minutes later, we've descended to a garage below my building's public space, gazing over a row of gleaming BMWs in different shades of gray and blue. As Emma takes it all in with a widening gape, I grin like a kid showing off his Lego collection. "Welcome to the nursery."

She swings her gaze around the garage and takes it all in. In this light, her eyes perfectly match the Long Beach blue of the M2 right behind her. "Excuse me?"

"One advantage of being in LA over New York, besides destiny's slam-dunk win this last week"—I clarify this with a wicked stare over her body—"has been indulging my little Bimmer addiction."

She giggles. "*Little*?"

"I blame my buyer. Shannon keeps finding me deals I can't pass up. She calls the machines her 'sweet babies.'"

"Ergo, the 'nursery.'"

"Bingo." I rub my hands together with eager joy. "So, which one do you want to play with?" I waggle my brows as she brightens the whole garage with her laughter. "How about the one that matches your eyes? She's cute—and fast."

She shakes her head and points to one of the M4 convertibles behind me. "I like going topless. The sun's about to set. Let's head for the beach."

I impale her with a mock frown. "Excuse me. I didn't hear a word you said after 'topless.'"

She snickers again. "Dork."

"*Your* dork."

A grin lights up her face as she gets into the passenger seat. "If you insist."

While waiting for the M4's roof to retract, I dip over the center console and yank her into an adamant kiss. "I insist."

Our hands stay entwined the whole trip to the coast.

Her idea was a damn good one. As we park at Pacific Palisades, the sun is just a gold disc on the horizon, still casting brilliant rays across the waves. The sand holds the heat of the day, and it surrounds our feet with grainy warmth as we make our way to the berm. We've stayed hand in hand. It still feels fucking amazing.

We walk to the edge of the berm and sit, butts in the softer sand and feet edging the firm moisture where the tide starts to tease. I release a satisfied sigh as Emma tilts her head onto my shoulder. Her sigh blends with the seagull caws and the rhythm of the waves. It's resonant with trust.

For right now, *this* space feels pretty okay.

More than okay.

"Reece?"

"Yeah?"

"Tell me if I'm overstepping...but since it *was* what sparked all the drama last night..."

I turn in, pressing lips to her forehead to indicate I'm able to fill in her implication. "I have no idea why Angelique's in LA, Velvet." I see a sailboat on the water, tacking south toward Marina Del Rey, and pray for the calm of its glide to permeate my tension. "She called out of the blue the day before last. Insisted on seeing me, that she had important shit to discuss with me."

With a sharp jerk, her head lifts. "Important shit like what?"

I expel a heavy breath. "I don't know. We never got that far."

She's still—too still—before murmuring, "How far *did* you get?"

"Up to the part where I tried giving the cufflinks back." I finally glance over, letting her see the pain I can't convey in my tone. "She gave them to me the night before—" A growled grunt. "Well, before everything changed." Then a rough chuckle. "They actually meant a lot to me at the time. When you have more money than everyone you date, there's an expectation *you'll* be buying the presents, you know? I was floored that someone had thought to get *me* something."

"Only to find out she wanted something from you after all."

"You could say that."

It's dry and bitter, but it's my truth. But even as she brings some comfort with the press of our foreheads, I can't set aside what I must say after that. *The fucked-up follow-up.* It's almost a hashtag. If only it weren't so goddamned necessary. So goddamned disgusting.

"And Emma..." I pull back a few inches, just to make sure she's really listening. "It's probably what she still wants from me."

Waves crash harder, ushering in the tide. A couple of seagulls fight for a corner of a trashed sandwich. Salt and smoke rush on the wind, changing midway from the balm of afternoon to the chill of night.

The woman next to me has gone eerily still again. "What do you mean?"

"Exactly what I'm saying." I press a hand to the side of her neck. "Angelique picked me up from the Brocade last night, presumably to go to dinner—but I got in the car and she instructed the driver to take us 'back to the house.' Not a restaurant. Not even another hotel. *The house.* Why would a woman passing through town be staying at a house?"

Emma frowns. "Maybe it belongs to a friend?"

"I assumed that too, but my gut told me differently. The blanks have been damn easy to fill in since then. It took my legal team about ten minutes to learn The Consortium's already filed for business licensing in the state. Their business address is a mansion on two acres out in Rancho Palos Verdes. I haven't dug any deeper than that, but I'm willing to bet the second owner on that place is Angelique La Salle."

She pulls away from my grasp. Pushing to her feet, she shakes out her head, turning her hair into white-gold streamers on the wind. "So what does all that mean?"

I scrub my face with both hands. Her crossed arms and hunched shoulders convey volumes of meaning. I've dropped so many damn bombs in the last few hours, and I'm about to pound her with one more—but like the others, this can't be helped.

"It means The Consortium is likely expanding their search for recruits into the States, targeting Los Angeles first."

Her shoulders visibly tighten. She drops her head, dipping it toward me without glancing all the way back. "Because of Bolt?"

"Probably," I mutter. "That, and a city full of people who already envision themselves as somebody like him."

"So what are we going to do?"

I reach for her and gently pull her back down. I coax her into my lap, where I can fill her mouth with a long, lingering, I'm-gonna-melt-the-hairs-off-your-toes kiss, which leaves us panting against each other's mouths.

Finally, I rasp, "Thank you."

"For what?" She's genuinely curious.

"For asking what *we're* going to do."

Her eyes go butter soft. She reaches her fingertips to my jaw and tenderly scrapes at my stubble. "I'm in this with you, Reece Richards." The edges of her lips kick up, emphasizing her adorable dimples. "Until you kick me off the boat, I'm in this thing through any storm that bitch wants to bring."

Riding a giant wave of feeling, I kiss her again—twice as long, doubly as deep. But her hands, one pulling in my hair and the other gripping my shoulder, compel me to touch her as well. Along her face. Down the curves of her breasts, her waist, her thighs, and then inward, teasing at the warm triangle between them.

She groans softly into my mouth. I growl determinedly back into hers. She tastes like sea salt and arousal. Smells like wind and sweat. *My* sweat. I want to drench her in it all over again. I need to feel her washed in me, confirming the truth Angelique stole from me.

I'm still human. I'm still me. I'm still passion and fire and need and feeling...

And love.

Holy shit. *Holy. Shit.*

I love her.

I should tell her.

But then what?

What if all my suspicions about The Consortium are true? Was that what Angelique wanted to meet with me about last night? To join their recruitment team here? And if I'd said no—translation, *hell fucking no, you deranged bitch*—what then? Would I have been dragged off to another secret rave somewhere? Is that still the fate that awaits me? After all this time, fighting some of the dirtiest criminal scum LA has thrown at me, am I still doomed to die on a gurney in a lab, fried by the lightning of my own blood?

If those bastards capture me again, it's a certainty. No guard will let the shackles slip on me this time.

And where will that leave the woman I've fallen ass over elbows for?

Pining for me, that's where. Wasting her life—a life meant for so much more—in madness, fruitlessly waiting for me to escape a life of being The Consortium's number one lab rat.

I won't do it to her. I can't.

But I know what I *can* do to her...

"Shit!" She exclaims it on a laugh as I reach up one leg of my shorts, which look a hell of a lot better on her than me, and swiftly find the trembling pearl of her desire. "Reece...*damn*." She quivers as I push back her intimate hood and pinch the hot ridge of her clit. "Wh-What...are you..."

"*We*," I correct her with a serrated growl. "You mean what are *we* going to do?" As I massage her clit, I lie back and swing her over to straddle me. Yeah, right here, in the middle of the beach. In the spell of the twilight. In the grip of everything I can only communicate to her in this way. Commanding her body, to prove how thoroughly she's conquered my heart.

"Oh. Kay." She bites her bottom lip to finish it, enticing me to kiss that stung cushion as I pull her down, molding her against me. "So...what are *we* going to do?"

I release a rickety breath and lift my gaze to meet the blue silk of hers. "Keep the sweatshirt pulled down," I instruct quietly. "Because I'm going to open my shorts and let my cock out. Then it's going to slide up inside you, and we're going to fuck like we can't get enough of each other."

"*Huh?*"

I slide a seductive smirk and caress her with heavy-lidded

seduction. "You telling me you've had enough of me, bunny? Because your pussy says otherwise."

She bites her lip harder. "Th-That's not it, and you know it."

"Then pull down the sweatshirt."

"Here?"

"Here."

"Now?"

The only answer I give is the grate of my zipper—and the surge of my dick. I owe her more of a churn than this. Romantic words and slow, wet kisses. Erotic imagery and flowery poetry. Sonnets and songs and fucking soliloquies about how she makes more than my blood glow—only now my blood *does* glow, so before I become the main attraction for the whole beach, I need to get my hands hidden beneath her clothes and my cock buried inside her sweet, silken body.

*Fuck. Her body.*

Her legs, tensing against mine as we begin to rock. Her cunt, such a tight, torrid channel around my swelling length. Even her back, with lithe muscles flexing against my grip as we thrust and writhe and climb together toward the ultimate, erotic burst.

But most of all, right now, her eyes.

Entrancing me like summer smoke. Drowning me like ocean depths. And with her fearless, dauntless desire, keeping me locked to her face as we surge together toward completion, giving me another gift I don't deserve but will greedily, thoroughly seize.

And completely, shamelessly, need.

*Her glow*—emanating from the best power source I've ever known or seen.

Her heart—my ultimate treasure.

The prize I can one day, somehow, be worthy of asking for in full.

Right now, I can only tell her that with the force of my own gaze and all the passion in my body—and hope it's enough.

*Dear God, let it be enough.*

# CHAPTER TWELVE

### EMMA

"The dude's getting laid."

"Has to be."

"Regularly."

"Definitely."

"Legit."

I stop where I'm at, in the doorway of the Brocade's break room, interrupting myself from my badass humming of *Believer*—I'm positive I'm going to make a billion dollars once Imagine Dragons hears this and demands I go on tour with them—to pay more attention to Wade and Fershan's back-and-forth.

"I mean, come *on*." Wade stabs chopsticks into his ramen and twirls the noodles in emphasis. "The Hagakure ramen bar today and Sandwich Heaven last Friday? Fresh flowers on all the tables in here?"

Fershan cocks a brow. "*Flowers* are what you notice? We both got instant cash bonuses for positive guest satisfaction."

"Which were whose idea to begin with?" I use the line while sliding between them to grab an edamame pod from the bowl they're sharing.

Fershan chuckles. "I officially bow to the queen of good ideas."

"Bows not necessary." I swipe a few more of the pods. "Just more of these, please." I moan while sucking out another of the tender green beans from their warm casing. "Damn. So good."

"Fine," Wade says. "Props to Em for the bonuses. But the rest of these bennies?" He swirls an empty chopstick in the air before stabbing it toward the hotel's main tower. "I'm sticking to my theory. Methinks, my friends, the weird one in yon gilded tower has been dipping his golden wick with blissful frequency."

"Ew." It's a fast way to disguise my furious blush, which I hide further by turning for the ramen bar. Though I could make a meal out of the edamame alone, I force myself to mull over the sauce choices while regaining my composure. Reece's little "gifts" for the team, sprinkled with care throughout the last two weeks, have meant more to me than jewelry, candy, or stuffed animals. As for the flowers? He's made sure they're part of my world every day—even here in the basement break room.

My hero. Sweeping me off my feet...in all the ways that matter.

"Forsooth." Fershan snickers while adding on to his friend's theory. "Methinks I doth agree with you. Our prince must be wooing a lady fair and extending his happiness to his people."

Wade groans. "Wooing? What the hell is that, man? *Wooing*?"

I toss a scowl over my shoulder. "A lot better than 'dipping his golden wick,' that's what."

"Whoa."

"Wade, the man's 'wick' is none of our—"

"No. I mean *whoa*."

The stab of shock in Wade's voice is a compulsion, causing me to pivot around as he snatches the remote to the break room's TV. As he scrolls the volume up, a heart-halting image consumes the screen. A muscled figure in black leather is leaping through the air like rockets are powering him.

Holy *wow*.

"Our dude's up and at it again," Wade exclaims. "Literally."

Fershan rises, dropping his chopsticks in favor of hoisting a hearty geek fist. "Oh, snap it up!" His eyes go wide. "Wait. Is that the power plant out at El Segundo?"

"Duh." Wade snorts.

"By the gods. What is he doing *there*?"

"Kicking ass, power-pulsing dickheads, and saving the city." Wade's tone implies the second *Duh*.

"In*deed*." Fershan skirts the table, intensifying the whoop-whoop fist. "Bolt, my man!"

*Actually...* I slip into a chair at the table behind theirs, smirking like a loon, as they both spin into fanboy mode. He's *my* man.

But in instances like this, I don't mind sharing. Not one damn bit. The only thing I *do* mind is throwing my own mask on. And, in many ways, I don a whole outfit to go with it. The guise is invisible but in place as blatantly as Reece's leathers and eye cover—a façade that allows me to *oooohh* and *ahhhh* along with everyone else but hold back the rest of what I feel when watching him jump, spin, battle, and bash with the body I've come to know, desire, and cherish.

And love.

Oh God, how I love him.

And oh God, are there moments when it sucks harder to mask

that fact. Like right now.

"Fucking bad*ass*," Wade exclaims.

"He's rocking it!" Fershan adds.

"You should see him with a finger vibe and some lube." My barely audible utterance is absorbed by the guys' excitement.

"He's rocking this shit."

"Rocking it out *loud*."

I smirk a little wider—and squirm a little more. My boyfriend's rocking this shit. Out loud. That means he'll have *a lot* of extra voltage to fry off tonight...

Lucky, lucky, *lucky* me.

But first, there's getting to watch him—how did Wade phrase it?—kick ass, power-pulse some bad guys, and save the city.

There's just one thing missing about that theory. Big-time.

I notice it at the same moment Wade and Fershan do.

"Where are...all the dickheads?" Fershan leans forward, asking it first.

Wade stands up. "He doesn't have any dickheads."

Fershan rises too. "Just a dick...girl?"

As I push to my feet, my heart plummets the opposite direction. It thuds in my stomach, exploding like a bad cold fusion science project, spreading shards of terror throughout my body. "N-Not a girl."

"Huh?"

I hardly hear Wade's comeback.

"Em? Are you all right?"

Or Fershan's anxious probe.

"Not. A. Girl." I seethe the words this time through my gritted teeth. "A bitch." I compel my feet to move, stumbling in front of them both. "A bitch he needs to kill."

I've never spoken such words before. But I've never been captive to such ruthless terror, which is worsening as the scene on the TV plays out even more. Only it's not a "scene." It's the truth, happening beyond my control and despite my horror.

The news station, only able to carry an aerial feed, shows Reece in full Bolt mode, dashing across ducts and roofs at the huge power plant across town, next to the ocean. Sure enough, it looks like he's chasing absolutely nothing, until the cameras pan to show another figure sprinting—with cascading blond hair, the legs of a stripper, and the boobs of a porn star. The whole damn world now knows this, thanks to Angelique's leather corset, matching mini skirt, and blood-red hip boots. Any shred of doubt I've had about her identity is erased by the sight of her upper back, where a red and black tattoo of angel's wings spreads from shoulder blade to shoulder blade.

Frankly, I don't care if the woman is sporting a tramp stamp and a genie girl outfit. She's throwing down one-on-one with the man I love on behalf of the criminals who kidnapped him, held him prisoner, and hijacked his bloodstream in the name of their higher science. They took his *life*—only to return now, ready to end it.

I don't know how else to interpret what I see Angelique doing to him.

For every energy pulse Reece throws, she has a comeback in the form of a giant shield, somehow connected to the force of the station itself, deflecting and then reflecting the punches. In strategic places, she stops to throw her weight on massive levers, unleashing smaller versions of what seem like electromagnetic pulses. As lights flicker, steam billows, and alarms blare, Reece crumples to the ground like a dog hit with a silent whistle. As soon as the pulse finishes, he gets back up, though he is visibly weakened by the smackdown.

My heart shoots to my throat. My mouth erupts with a terrified moan. I grab the edge of the table, the only thing preventing my knees from crumpling. But what good will that do? What good can *I* do at all? I can't be there next to him, as my soul yearns. I can't run to him, help him, be there for him. I can't even yell at him to get up, as Wade and Fershan can. What if I lose my shit and spill his name? I can only watch, clutched by the same mortification as the rest of the city, as a female dressed like a Santa Monica hooker and moving like a million-dollar action star keeps driving their super hero to his knees.

After the fourth electromagnetic pulse, Reece can no longer struggle to his feet. He unfurls from the fetal position and rolls to his back, dusty and defeated. I stagger closer to the TV, unable to stop the tears from rolling down my cheeks and the air from pounding in and out of my lungs, despite my attention being fixed on someone else's chest... On any sign of life from the man I love, still sprawled on the ground in a hailstorm of power station sparks, fighting to accept he has, at last, been defeated.

I sense it even as I watch him from this distance, through this impartial lens. Hell, maybe the news cameras make me see it better, sense it deeper. It's as if I'm soaring in there next to him. I almost know what he's thinking just by watching him...

He's giving up.

"No," I rasp.

Preparing himself for the inevitable.

"No!"

Defeat is written in the rigid set of his head. The fists formed at the ends of both arms. The pallor of his skin, noticeable even from the altitude at which the helicopter hovers.

"*No!*"

Any moment now, Angelique will appear at his side, gloating like a triumphant Deneuve, missing only her Balenciaga tote and her fancy French cigarette. Doubtful she'll be toting a glass of water for her new captive either.

Unless...

The glass of water finds a way to the party anyway.

Unless...

The miracle for which I've just given up hope is delivered by the angels themselves, in the form of mist that turns to rain. Inside a minute, the concrete slab under Reece becomes a solid wet sheen.

And then one of the loose power lines flies over, touches down, and ignites the slab with blinding ribbons of electricity.

Shooting the man I love straight into the dark sky.

*Shit, shit, shit, shit.*

"Fuccckkkker!" Wade shouts.

"*Booooyaaaaahhh!*" Fershan yelps.

"Reece!" It detonates from me in the same instant. I'm beyond caring. I can only spin and race where I dropped my purse, diving into the thing for my cell. Once it's in my grip, I can't get to the speed-dial list fast enough. Tears blur my vision, and I cuss as I tap on the wrong window. Calling the dry cleaners for a rush job right now is the last thing on my mind. Summoning Zalkon for the same thing? As Reece would say—Bingo.

*Reece.*

His name is the only thing I allow into my mind. The only thrum of importance. The only thought that matters. And yeah, that includes how my two coworkers follow every inch of my movements like kittens after a laser, finally finding their opening in the forever it seems to take Z to pick up my call.

"The hell?" Wade blurts.

"Krishna's balls," Fershan gasps.

"Not now," I snap at them both.

"But—"

"But—"

"Not. *Now.*" I leave the room with the phone locked to my ear. The second Z picks up, a smartass one-liner prepped to fling through the line, I interrupt him too. "Reece needs us. Don't even bother with getting me at the front of the hotel. I'll meet you at the employee entrance. *Hurry!*"

### R E E C E

"Wh-What the hell?" I mutter. "*Where* the hell—"

"Ssshhh."

In the chaos I used to call my senses, this woman's voice is the only thing of worthy clarity. It cuts through the raging voltage in my blood, the flooded capacitors of my muscles, the torched circuits of my brain. "Emma?"

"*Sssshhh.*"

"Fuck." I fight to push up. "C-Can't stop, Velvet. Not now. Angelique—"

"Is gone." She says it simply, but there's a terrified wobble beneath it. Her fear isn't ribbons. It's gigantic ropes, holding her back. No. Holding her *in*. She's keeping her shit together. For me? Why?

I stow that question in favor of the easier one to answer.

"Dead?"

I'm not proud of the bald hope in the cold word. Angelique told me enough about her life that I believed, and still do, in some kind of good tucked deeply inside her. More than that, I'm an asshole, not a murderer. But with everything else in my system fried, I can't help tossing my filters into the fire too.

"We don't know." Her tone still shakes, though I barely hear it as a huge truck rumbles by. I gather enough of my senses to realize I'm lying in two inches of mud in a shallow ditch halfway between the power station and the road.

"Holy shit," I mutter.

"No kidding." The interjection belongs to Zalkon, braced a few feet behind Emma. His tie is loose, mud spatters his black suit, and freaked-the-hell-out is written all over his swarthy face.

"There was an electrical burst." Dots of mist outline Emma's profile as she eyes the power station, now crawling with police, firemen, and energy company reps. "A live power line came down on the wet cement, and—"

"I remember." At least I think I do. It's hard to think straight. My brain is a ball of pain. The careening lights of the emergency crews are red and blue lances on my throbbing gray matter. "Damn. I must have been thrown all the way over the fence."

Emma smooths a chunk of hair back from my forehead with shaky fingertips. "Do you remember anything else? What happened before that?"

"Yeah." It's dark, and I'm still fifty kinds of dizzy, but I fumble a hand up to grasp hers. "Mostly." As shitty as I feel about it, I borrow her warmth, which lends me strength to speak. "I got a ping on my police scanner and couldn't ignore it. They said there was a break-in at the plant. Some person was packing serious heat, looking like they were going to fuck with the city's power grid."

Emma stiffens. "And it was her."

"Yeah."

"Knowing exactly how she could fuck with *you* in that environment."

"Yeah." I feel like a bigger asshole when she violently shivers, right before her composure breaks on a messy sob. Desperately, I pull her down, absorbing the flood of her grief with my shoulder. "Hey. *Hey,* beauty, it's okay."

She twists a hand into my hair and detonates a new sob against my neck. "It's not okay!"

"Emma?" Z steps back over.

I shoot him a thank-you-but-stay-away look, soothing my protective caveman but screwing my reformed douchebag. I have no right to be holding her like this. Fuck, I hardly *can* hold her like this. My arms feel like noodles. My brain's still filled with excruciating fuzz.

While I know the drain on my system is temporary, the implications in my life aren't. Never has a moment been more symbolic of that truth than now. She should be at home tonight with a man like—well, like Z. A good guy in a nice suit, with a steady job and ready humor. Someone who will always be there for her, not a drained sap in a ditch, offering her nothing but agony, tears, and mud.

"I'm fine." Her protest is watery but determined. She pushes up, squaring her shoulders. "*I'm fine.* But I swear to God, if Angelique La Salle ever *thinks* she can come near you again—"

I cut into her rant with a hard squeeze to her forearm. "Then I'll be more prepared than I was tonight."

"Who's Angelique La Salle?"

"Bet your hot ass you'll be prepared." My girl rocks her head with more swagger than a rapper, stabbing her free hand into the air. "You'll be prepared with me at your side, ready to show her bad pleather and hip waders with heels only work on desperate johns in Santa Monica."

Z goes silent. Clearly, he's not sure whether to laugh, growl, or high-five my girl. I'm in the same boat—technically, mired in the same ditch—only with one more available option, which I readily grasp.

I kiss her.

Then again.

Then a third time, letting our lips linger longer, taste deeper, twine tighter. I groan hard, drinking in her strength like a damn vampire, especially as the force of her passion works its way into the electrons of my blood, the power cells of my spirit, the fiber of my muscles.

And in that moment, I know.

I'll never be able to live without her.

Which is why I *must* live without her.

Never has a decision felt more right—or more shitty—in my life. It hits my heart like a sea change and moves mountain ranges in my mind. It feels catastrophic and cataclysmic, but destined...and determined. When I figure out why, I bark out a soft laugh.

I've just made a choice not involving a shred of my own needs.

"Reece?" My reaction hasn't been lost on Emma. She subjects me to her anxious scrutiny, her hands furtively feeling my face. "What is it?"

"You mean, other than the fact that h-he's..." Z's voice disappears on a stunned stutter.

"Ready to fire on torpedo bay one?" I laugh again, waving my glow stick digits as if to zap him. "Guess the boss *is* a fun guy now, huh?"

An easy grin spreads across Z's rugged face. "Just tell me where the Death Star is and we'll blast off, sir."

I roll to my feet as my strength starts regenerating. The electrons, zooming through me like a squadron of fighters zooming at their own Death Star, send me sprinting toward the Mercedes. With Emma still so close, I float an educated guess about what quadrant of the universe for which they're hitting the warp-speed switches. "Now that you know the classified shit, I'll have to kill you."

Z, keeping pace with me until now, halts in the sludge with a loud *slup*. "Errr—"

"Kidding."

"Thank fuck," he mutters.

"Thank God," Emma rasps at the same time. In the second I take to frown down at her, standing in the space between the car's door and back seat, she darts a nervous glance up through her lashes. "Because I *might* have been a little stressed when the news outlets broadcasted your showdown with Angelique..."

"And?" I prompt.

"And...I might have told Wade and Fershan about you too."

Zalkon, standing next to the driver's seat, snickers. "Which, in those guys' minds, really did turn you into the coolest boss on the planet."

Emma giggles. "No argument here."

I lean down, kissing the playful tilt on her lips. "Even if I decide they have to be killed too?"

"Oh, no." She blinks wide doll eyes. "Not *that*, Mr. Richards."

"Well..." My stare dips down the length of her body. "Maybe I can accept your penance for it."

Her gaze flares. "My *penance*?"

"Mmmhmmm." I nod with lascivious languor. "I'll take it out of you...in flesh."

"Oh. In *that* case." She topples backward onto the seat, yanking me into the car after her. I barely drag the door closed before Z has the motor gunned and the car in motion, lurching my lips onto hers through the sheer magic of Newton's first law.

I keep letting my mouth fall over hers. I bite her and dominate her and sweep into her, roaring my tongue into the dark, hot cavity of her, plunging in a simulation of what my cock's about to do to her pussy. She groans her acknowledgement, reaches her hands for my neck, and lets me continue to fill and possess her mouth.

"Z." I raise my voice at the guy but don't look away from her. "Put up the barrier."

Emma's mouth twitches. She lifts a leg, thunking one of her pumps against the sliding door between us and the front seat. She giggles again as her shoe falls off, clunking to the car's floor. "Looks like he already did."

"Good man."

She shrugs, a good excuse for bringing her hands to the front of her button-up blouse. "He works for the coolest boss on the planet. Of course he's a good man."

I watch her fingers, mesmerized with every new inch of alabaster skin she exposes, especially as the lace of her bra comes into view. But the recognition hits, hard and violent, that this *will* be the last time I'm with her like this. Gazing at her open and exposed like this. A spell only begun with her physical perfection...

But what an amazing place to start.

"I'm not a good man, Emma."

The growl unfurls from my throat as I push my hands up her legs and grip her black pantyhose with my fingernails, ready to rip them with rough urgency—only to learn the hose are actually thigh-high stockings secured to her legs with a sexy-as-fuck garter belt. At the center is a tiny triangle of black satin that, in some crazy alternate universe, can be called underwear.

My breath snags in my throat. I snap my stare back toward her face. Her smile of impish seduction already awaits. "Well, what do you know?" She swings her other leg out, raising it over my shoulder. "*I'm* not good either, Mr. Richards."

Before I can help it, a laugh erupts from the depths of my belly—and the core of my soul. *This woman.* This incredible, unforgettable creature. The lightning in my blood might be responsible for how I met her, but the storm she's left in my heart will never, ever subside.

I let that secret confession take hold of my mind while compelling my hands to shove the panties from her gorgeous cleft.

"My sweet, shiny surprise." I slide a finger in, trailing through her trembling folds from top to bottom.

"Thought you'd like it." She rests her head back against the car's door while lifting her chin with sensual invitation. "I got them online. It was a little weird putting them on in the bathroom at work, but they made me think of you the rest of the day."

I stroke her again, deliberately zeroing in on her clit. "I'm glad you did."

Her hips buck. Her lips fall open. "Maybe I should get a few more."

And maybe I need to change the subject. Fast.

Hating the fuck out of myself as I do.

Maybe I shouldn't lend a hand in destroying *this* set.

*I am not a good man, Emma.*

If I were, I wouldn't be pushing out her leg a little more, absorbing the heady sight of her pussy, wet and waiting and spread and slick. I wouldn't be whipping at the fastenings of my leathers with such primal urgency, groaning as my dick surges out in readiness. I wouldn't be positioning myself at her dark slit, working my rigid bulb between her waiting lips, lubing the opening with my burning drips of pre-come.

If I were anything close to a good man, the nasty words in my mind wouldn't be turning into filthy promises on my lips. "It's time for your penance, Emmalina—and I'm going to exact it by fucking your cunt raw."

Her whole frame shakes. Her lungs, pumping heavily, push her breasts into her waiting hands. She claws aside the edges of her bra from the middle out, baring herself in a wild rending, a la the most famous super hero move on earth—with a twist that's uniquely, erotically hers.

Sassy, gorgeous siren.

Sexy, incredible super heroine.

Mine. Mine. Mine.

If only for this last, ill-gotten collection of moments...*mine*.

The sight of her naked tits, plucked and abused by her own greedy hands, drives my sanity past the edge of control. I surge forward, stretching her pussy with one push of my full erection. I fuck her so full and hard and deep, she sighs and shudders and screams with the force of me.

"You want more, Velvet?"

"Yes. *Yes.*"

Gladly, I give it to her. Over and over and over again.

"More?"

"Yes! More of your cock. Please, Reece!"

"You want this cock to make you come?"

"*Fuck.*" She whips her head from left to right and back again, consumed by erotic ecstasy.

"I asked you a question, Emmalina."

"Y-Yes," she manages. "Damn it, yes. I want your cock to make me come!"

"Then do it." I roll into her, scraping her exposed nub with the pressure of my abdomen. "*Do it,*" I order through locked teeth, even as I feel her thrumming around my dick, milking me with the force of her release.

Pulling the orgasm out of me too. Taking it all from me. Taking all that *is* me.

Until more astounding words form on my lips.

"I love you, Emmalina Crist."

A song bleeds over from Z's playlist in the front seat. The guy's into every icon of classic rock, meaning David Bowie's voice doesn't come as a surprise—nor does the song. Perhaps it's the rightness I feel about this moment. The recognition that this *is* the choice, at last, of a super hero—no matter how fucking hard it's going to be, especially after just slapping my heart on my fucking sleeve.

Especially as the song ramps up more. Bowie sings, in his Bowie way, about nothing but everything mattering. About forever and ever existing in one day.

"I love you too, Reece Richards."

Her admission doesn't shock me—but it doesn't make me feel great. Not as great as I'd expected. Her voice is a sparse rasp on the words...as if they make her more sad than joyous. As if she agrees with the bittersweet ache of Bowie's croon, blending its dystopian feel with the rumble of the wheels on the freeway. I pull my body from hers as the song talks of guns and kisses, of a king and a queen... and of becoming heroes...

She turns so I'm embracing her from behind. I already hate feeling this detached from her, though bitch-slap myself for the mush. Do I want to know that she's close or safe? What would have happened if she'd been anywhere close to me in El Segundo? What would Angelique have done to take Emma out of the picture—out of *my* picture—in a remote location like that?

I refuse to focus on the answer to that. I'll accept tonight as the easier way to learn that lesson—and I'll do it with gratitude.

Our silence continues as downtown's distinctive landscape

looms closer. The circle-shaped tops of the US Bank and 777 Towers. The proud obelisks of the Aon Center and Union Bank Plaza. The huge purple dome of the arena at LA Live, and the City Hall building used in hundreds of films and TV shows.

And tucked between them all, the stylized gold tower of the Brocade.

The moment the hotel slides into view, the woman in my arms releases a weighted breath. Again, she doesn't sound happy. More like...resigned.

And sorrowed.

"You're getting out there, aren't you?" The same conflict crowds her soft challenge. "At the Brocade." She presses a hand to my chest, as if the move will give her a temperature reading on my heart. As if *that* will work—or tell her that what my heart wants right now isn't what I can give it.

"Emma—"

"Just answer me, damn it." Her voice thickens as if tears are about to break through, though her eyes are dry as desert skies. "You're going to get out, ride up to that penthouse, and shut out the world, me included, like you have for the last goddamned year, all because of your idiotic fear—"

"Idiotic?" I push away. I stuff my cock back into my leathers and refasten them. If she wants fear, I'll give it to her. "You were watching tonight, right?" I charge. "You said you were."

"If I said I watched, I watched." The syntax is defensive, but her tone goes far beyond. She's clearly pissed. Good. Maybe pissed is where I need her to be so she'll clear the love out of her ears and listen.

"So you saw what Angelique tried to do to me?" I snarl. "What would have happened if you'd been there with me? What would have happened if we were just out on a date together, instead? What's *going* to happen if she ever finds out I've split the sidewalk falling this hard in love?"

Her lips quirk, despite her obvious effort to control the knee-jerk at my metaphor. "You think I don't know how to handle the sidewalk, even *with* Angelique on it?"

I steel my jaw. "I think you don't understand The Consortium. They're not some fringe band of radicals with a weird scientific hair up their ass, Emma. They're cold, they're methodical, and they're ruthless—and I'm the loose thread in their ugly orange sweater. They're determined to sew me back into the thing or cut the thread loose, including any other threads that are now attached to it. It's a no-win game, and I've been just fucking fine with letting them come after me for that win—"

"Until now," she supplies dismally.

"Yeah." I finally unclench my teeth enough to talk again. "Until now." I slide my grip back into her hair. I crush her brilliant strands with the intensity of my fist, gulping while imagining *her* sprawled on a sidewalk, killed in the name of The Consortium's crazy quest. "It's not going to happen," I vow. "It's *not* going to happen."

She lifts her head to fervently search my face. "So what are you going to do?"

"I'm taking myself out of it. *And* you. Fuck. *Especially* you."

I enforce it by yanking her up and kissing her hard. God*damn*, she still tastes so good. And feels even better. She compels my mouth back to hers with an aching whimper, her fingers twining in my hair.

She pulls to the point of pain, accelerating my blood from the heady rush. I can't refuse the stab of her tongue any more than I can turn down air. We make out like that, hot and horny as teenagers at the beach, Bowie still crooning as Z exits the freeway and winds through the noisy avenues of downtown.

When we part, taking in huge gulps of air, that sad sound flows from her again. She launches at me, clutching hard, begging in a whisper against my neck.

"Don't." Her nails dig ruthless half-moons into my nape. *"Don't,* Reece...*please."*

I wrap my arms around her. Inhale her, all rain and honey and grief, and force out my answer. "I have to."

"You never *have* to hide."

I duck my head against her hair and shake it slowly. "Right now, hiding is beating them."

"Hiding is losing to them! Damn it, if—"

She chokes into silence as soon as my fist rams the car's window. The reinforced pane is a sudden burst of textures, almost resembling stained glass as the shards reflect the colors of the city. That's the pretty way of looking at it—and maybe that's best, since the air in the car fills with hard truth and uncomfortable acceptance.

A couple of minutes later, Z rolls the car to a stop beneath the lonely awning of my private entrance to the hotel. I suck in a huge breath and shove it back out, trying to reconsider her words. *Is* there another way, or do I have to be *that* brand of douchebag too? Yeah, the one who just screwed his girl with the full intention of leaving her afterward. The one who told her he loved her somewhere in that mess.

The one who's now going to leave this car yearning to touch her once more in some small way, but instead ordering myself to get out with barely a glance backward. Taking one more breath. Fighting through one more second, which will be like the other disgusting seconds, torturous minutes, agonizing hours, and miserable days of the lonely weeks and years to come.

"Send me a bill for the window, Z."

"Of course, Mr. Richards."

"I love you, Emmalina."

"Fuck you, Mr. Richards."

# CHAPTER THIRTEEN

## EMMA

Damn him.

*Damn him*, anyway.

I've only heard of this kind of sorrow before. To be honest, I thought it didn't really exist. What kind of heartbreak dives so deep into a person they can't even shed tears because of it? Anything a person spends life on is worth spending grief on too, right? And that means tears, right?

But the hours after he leaves become a day.

That day becomes two.

Then three.

And every day, the grief comes back. I hope, of course, that because there are no tears, it didn't mean as much to me as I'd originally thought. That *he* didn't mean as much.

At times, I come close to believing that. Like when work gets busy, despite Wade and Fershan treating the floor three feet around me like holy ground. Or in those magical moments when I'm lost in a good book, or even when something interesting on the train distracts me, yanking me out of the solitude known as my heart.

In those tiny and treasured moments, I start to think everything is normal again—just before it all returns. The memories. The aching. The loss, in places so far and awful inside me, no food will stay down, thought will stay planted, or feeling will take root. The limbo of this damn darkness. The pain still so deep, I even start to hope for the tears now. Any sign the sorrow will turn to healing soon.

On that "cheerful" thought, I pack up the last of my snacks and water bottle for work, tuck them into my shoulder satchel, and set off from the apartment to catch the three p.m. train.

While walking down the two flights of stairs to the courtyard, I think about the new day-shift slots that have recently opened in the office. I revisit the idea of requesting to take one of them, just for a little while.

Maybe more than a little while.

It's a temporary fix, but maybe that's what I need to escape the Reece-themed slap I endure every night at the Brocade. Neeta was actually the one who mentioned the new shifts, sensing my struggles and perhaps even guessing Reece is the root of the problem.

But would I just be replacing one Pandora's box with another? Right now, at night, I only have to deal with memories of him. What will I do if I'm actually forced to see him, which is much more a possibility during standard business hours?

Especially because I know how he's been spending his evenings lately.

Oh, yes. Bolt sightings are on the rise again. The whole city couldn't be more ecstatic.

Goodie for the city.

On that morose thought, I plunk to the bottom of the stairs.

Once there, I stop and give those ruminations an open huff. "And here she is, folks. The most depressed girl in the world's safest city. Give it up for...Emmalina Crissssttt."

As I finish my fake crowd noises, I scowl. Damn. I just used my own full name on myself.

*The way Reece does.*

*The way Reece used to.*

"Well, at least you *look* runway ready, baby." I reward myself for the pep talk with a soft laugh directed toward the bow-front kitten heels upon which I splurged as my heartbreak shoes. They've been sitting in the box for two days, but their Kelly-green color meant I had to wait for the ideal blouse to come back from the dry cleaners. Tonight, the whole ensemble has come together. I may not feel totally rockin'-red-carpet again, but at least I look it.

"Did I miss the punch line?"

So much for considering steps on a red carpet—or *any* steps at all—as I swing a glower toward the source of the quip. The line is as friendly as a greeting from one of my neighbors—if any of them had a Catherine Deneuve accent and smelled like Baccarat perfume mixed with clove cigarettes. But the scent isn't what lodges my heart in my throat. I'm not even struck senseless by the fear Reece warned me to be so nutballs about—which is disconcerting but not entirely disturbing.

Because I like what I feel in fear's place.

I let the rage settle in, pure and invigorating, while glaring at the bitch from head to toe. When I'm done with the onceover, I let out another laugh. Louder this time. And so much longer.

"Angelique La Salle." I rock back on one foot. "The woman

with the name of a princess and the wardrobe of a skank. Should I congratulate you on being well-rounded or just a puppet ho?"

The woman adopts a similar pose, her lips hitching like a droll doll. For a flash of a second, I catch something else on her face too. It's the dread Reece kept warning *me* about—and it almost makes me feel sorry for the woman. For half a second.

Then I'm right back to hating the woman.

I only have to remember her sending Reece to his knees at the power station, adding humiliation to her initial betrayal. Deepening the sorrow that convinced him to never believe in the word *trust* again.

In so many ways, this bitch has already killed the man I love.

"Puppet ho." She issues the echo with a mirthful half smile. "That is...*très créatif*, I will grant you that." Her head tilts. "Hmmm. I see it now, a little bit, I think."

"See what?"

"The quality you have...that captivates Reece."

"Captivat*ed* Reece. Past tense. I haven't seen the man in three days." I'm thankful I'm able to fling it and mean it. Thankful to the tune of considering calling in sick tonight and replacing the work hours with copious wine consumption and a trash-TV binge.

Shit. Surreal second number two. Have I just understood a little of what made Reece cut things off with me the other night?

*The...Consortium...is...cold...methodical...ruthless...*

For three days, I've been stewing about him being a pussy, choosing to hide from them with the grander excuse of protecting me. But right now, I'm damn relieved *I'm* able to shield *him*.

"Haven't 'seen' him, or haven't *seen* him?"

"Okaaaaayy." I'm still grateful she's getting only my gut-level truth—meaning my genuine confusion. "You have hidden cameras in the bushes, right?" I peer into the bougainvillea, using the moment to disguise my next emotion. Pure triumph. *I don't know where Reece is—but neither do they.*

"Are you able to answer the question?" As she takes a couple of deliberate steps forward, she reaches into hidden pockets in both her boots—releasing matching switchblades from the hidden compartments. She triggers the blades simultaneously, *thwacking* the steel on the air. The knives gleam in the afternoon sun as she advances with steadier purpose.

For two seconds, I indulge the folly of being concerned.

And then use my lunch pouch to knock one of them free and my water bottle to rid her of the other. Yeah, just like that, watching her scramble to scoop them up, pressing my lips to keep from laughing. I try to remember Reece's warnings about the bitch, but rage has taken over, blinding me to common sense. The only thing I can think about is giving this Twinkie an LA-style version of karmic payback.

As she crouches lower for the second knife, I land a kitten heel in the center of her spine and dig in to knock her forward. She rolls over, but I've got kitten heel number two at the ready, and I jam it deep enough into her windpipe to ensure she gets the message.

"You ready for my answer now, darling? I haven't seen Reece in at least three days, nor do I plan on seeing him again. But if I *did*, I'd be advising him to run like hell from a woman who doesn't have the sense to trash a pair of boots like that after the whole city saw her on every news feed in town trying to take down their most beloved local hero and a chunk of LA's power supply."

I finally release my foot. Angelique lurches to her feet and grabs at her throat, choking out stuff in guttural French while running for the street and disappearing around the curve in the road. I'm pretty sure she called me either a raving bitch or a bowl of soup, though I'd bank on the former. I'm also pretty sure there's a car waiting for her around that bend, and I should chase her to take notes or other super spy stuff like that, but I wouldn't bet on my knees carrying me another step, let alone into a Bond girl chase scene. On top of that, every drop of adrenalin in my body now migrates to both ends of it. My head becomes a tornado. My feet quiver like I've strapped them to shake weights. The guts in between are a directionless mess.

Miracle of miracles, I'm able to climb the stairs to my unit without tripping. Aligning my apartment key with the little hole in the door? Not even a miracle's going to help now.

"Emmalina."

I whirl—to behold a walking, talking, six-foot-three miracle.

No. A blade of lightning. A force of nature. The heir with the hair. The billionaire bad boy. The sexy asshole in the spire.

My Bolt.

My man.

"Oh." The syllable is all I can produce, my voice high and hurting but joyous and jubilant, as I fly into his arms without restraint or regret.

He lets out an, "Oof!" before laughing as I circle both legs around his waist, letting him take the keys and work my apartment lock open.

We move inside.

And I'm home. Really home.

Right where I need to be—after three damn days of hell.

*Three days.* Seventy-two hours. Anyone else would say they're blips in the span of time, but I call everyone else freaking crazy.

"Oh...wow." As I gasp it out, he drenches me in one of his lush laughs. I dive again for him, kissing him like crazy.

As my tears finally fall.

As I flood him with them, unashamed about turning the front of his dark-blue T-shirt into a piece of cobalt pop art.

As he returns the passion, trailing kisses through my hair.

He feels *so good.* His embrace is perfect, powerful, complete. I can feel his heartbeat mating with mine in our triumphant homecoming.

No.

This isn't a reunion. It can't be.

Nothing is different. Nothing has been fixed. As a matter of fact...

"What the *hell*?" I shove away from him and race around the room, slamming the blinds shut. "Oh my God, Reece, you can't be here. Angelique—"

"I know."

"Huh?"

"I know. She was here."

"You..."

"I've been tracking her."

"You've been *what*?" I spin around, grabbing him by both forearms. "How?"

He blushes. Holy *shit*. The man is even hotter in blushing, bumbling mode than he is in alpha demigod mode. "Easy, really.

Just checked signatures for all cell phones on site at the El Segundo power plant on Friday night and ruled out the devices belonging to employees and me. Once I pinpointed her phone, it was easy to—"

"Okay, okay." I giggle. "I get the gist."

He doesn't match my laugh this time. He twists our hold so he's got *me* by the forearms, cradling my elbows while his gaze holds me like silver angel wings.

"I've been tracking her everywhere she goes. She's mostly been back and forth from the mansion The Consortium's surel form once again. His face ignites with something like awe, and his g enerous mouth spreads in a wide smile. "No. Not incredible. Magnificent." He pushes into my personal space, cupping the back of my neck, and takes my mouth in a tender kiss. "You became *my* Bolt, Emmalina Crist."

I moan in soft delight when he repeats the kiss with more demand, suckling his way into my mouth. Every cell in my body blazes to new life. I can tell he's on the exact same page when his blue and gold fingertips flare in my peripheral, but I push back, ordering my hormones to stand down.

"I'm proud that *you're* proud, Mr. Richards, but we're still back at the same place we were before." I sigh heavily. "Maybe even worse, since I now understand how The Consortium really doesn't know the meaning of the word boundaries."

He dips a terse nod. "Yeah. Definitely worse."

He steps away completely, starting to methodically pace the room with hands on his lean hips. I take just a second to admire the view. The tailored black slacks he wears with the T-shirt fit his ass as perfectly as any pair of jeans ever, perhaps even better.

"This won't be the last time Angelique decides to make a house call," he goes on. "I guarantee The Consortium will pick up *some* vibe that you're still in contact with me."

"And being apart completely is *off* the table."

"On more levels than the obvious." He flashes a wink over his shoulder.

A long pause goes by, thickening with our combined tension. Not so jokingly, I mutter, "Maybe there's a remote island in the South Pacific somewhere. A cute hotel where everyone pays in puka shells and smiles? I could wear a muumuu to work every day..."

"Uh-uh." Reece saunters back over and tugs me into the perfect envelope of his embrace. "Wrong direction. You need to find a place where work attire is just the shells and the smile."

I help out with the smile part, at least. After we kiss softly, I sigh against his chest, treasuring the sound of the steady thumps beneath my ear. "We'll figure this out."

"*I'll* figure this out." He presses his lips into the top of my head. "I got you into this crazy mess, Emmalina."

"I *like* the crazy mess—as long as I'm in it with you, okay?"

"Okay." He lowers his head, fitting his forehead to mine. "Trust me?"

"Always."

♦ ♦ ♦ ♦

Three days later, *always* is getting a little harder to keep believing.

Those are my exact words in a text message to Reece, snuck in during a trip to the ladies' room that I can hopefully stretch out for another minute without suspicion. I've purposely picked the facilities farthest from the ballroom at the Pelican Hill Resort, hoping Mother, Father, and Lydia decide to forget where I am. If I'm lucky, maybe I can pass the next hour here in my cozy stall, smelling the "tropical flowers" being automatically spritzed into the air and trading messages with the man who's turned sexting into an art.

The same way he's turned over every inch of my heart.

I love him. I can't stop telling him. Because he's the only one who ever gets to know.

Ahhh, the fantasy life of a super hero's girlfriend.

I text something close to that, giggling softly at his reply.

*Well. I specialize in fantasies, Miss Crist.*

*You're just hard-up, Mr. Richards.*

*For you, Miss Crist.*

*Oh yeah? And when was the last time you were in the penis-crushing hell of Orange County?*

*More recently than you think.*

*Now this sounds interesting...*

I'm settling in for a juicy story when the bathroom door creaks open.

"Emmalina? Are you in *this* bathroom?"

I grit my teeth, fighting the temptation to scream at Mother's summons—a wasted endeavor even if I did indulge. Screaming doesn't help when it comes to my family. They love me, in their shrouded way. *Deeply* shrouded.

"Right here." I force civility to the response. It's not her fault that I can't seem to jump on the Newport-Beach-is-complete-nirvana boat. I've given up on even finding the dock. "I'm almost done."

"Oh, good." She makes primping sounds from the bathroom's vanity area. "Dinner will be served in a while, and then they'll start the awards ceremony—but you're missing all the fun stuff."

"Of course."

My forced pleasantry might pass acting muster with anyone but Laurel Crist. In two seconds, her maternal lasers pierce right through my sham.

"Honestly, Emma." She rises as I emerge, folding arms over her St. John crinkle silk picot gown. She's wearing matching heels and gemstone earrings, all meant to highlight the eyes that nearly match mine in color. "You're in the hospitality industry. You need to be more...hospitable."

"I *am* hospitable—to my guests." I smile, squeezing out a little charm—especially when pondering how my primped, perfect mother would react if knowing how *charming* I've just been with Reece freaking Richards. But that's not a truth she gets to know. Not a secret the world will ever discover.

"Can you just say you'll try, missy?"

I take a Zen breath, gritting to continue the smile. "Yes, ma'am."

"And put on some darker lipstick. You look washed out."

I deflect that one the best way I know how. "*You* look super pretty tonight."

"Really?" She skips a look backward. "You think so? Does this cut make my hips look—"

"You look stunning." Though I mean it, I can see she doesn't believe me. She eyes herself in the full-length mirror, her stare critical.

"Your father told me to wear navy." She *tsks* and shakes her head. "He thinks I look jaundiced in this."

I reach and grab her hand. "Well, he's wrong."

"You say the nicest things, honey." She pats the side of my face. "But you still need a darker shade of lipstick. Maybe your sister will have something you can borrow."

We reenter cocktail reception hell. I hide out in my typical place, at Lydia's side, letting my tennis star sister bask in the smooches, air kisses, and half hugs from people here to see her. Actually, the affection stuff isn't so bad. It's the conversation between all of it, centering around the same twelve subjects, that makes me wonder if a person can truly slit their wrists with a butter knife.

At times, I do try to engage—only to be greeted with the same glassy-eyed expressions in response to any of the tidbits I get hounded to share.

"Ohhhh. You're living in *downtown* LA? Why?"

"But there are so many adventures right here. I mean, have you *seen* the new yogurt place?"

"Why do you work the night shift? Aren't you good enough for the day one?"

"What movie stars have you met? Or do they get handled by the normal hotel workers?"

"You take the train to work? Well, what's wrong with your

driving?"

*What's wrong with you?*

My teeth lock, freezing my smile in place. My hands clench behind my back. My head starts to pound, and I fight an insane craving to jump out the window.

*What's wrong with you?*

I should be used to the refrain by now, right? Then why does it seem more relentless now? Why does it weigh on every breath I take and move I make, closing in like the inside of a grand, pretty box? *But why would you want more than this? Isn't the box enough? Why do you want to be more, when you have this?*

I find my place setting and sit down to watch the frozen butter rosettes start to melt, wondering when they'll stop looking like flowers—and feel weirdly sad for when they do. People don't like butter as much when it doesn't look like a rose. But doesn't it taste the same?

Yep. It's official. I really *am* in hell.

Except suddenly, hell comes to a complete stop.

An all-consuming hush—interrupted by waves of fervid whispers. Then astonished gasps. Then high outcries. Even a few elated little old lady *yeep*s.

Lydia appears at my side. Her face reflects the same stunned curiosity as everyone else's. "Holy *shit*, Em."

"Holy shit what?" I scrutinize her. "'Dia? Are you—what the hell?"

"Stand *up*." She titters a little, urging me to my feet. Doesn't take much effort. She's been playing tennis for nearly twelve years and her arms are like Mack Truck pistons. "Stand *up*, girl. Ohmigod, what's he doing here?"

"He who?"

"I'm going to pass out. This is epic."

"*What* is?"

*Epic.* Well, that's one way of saying it. Breathtaking could be another. Beautiful, too. But no matter how many descriptors I add to the mix, they don't come close to the twist of my stomach, the leap of my pulse, the race of my blood, and the lightning in my heart as a flawless figure in black leather strides across the room like he owns it. Who knows? Maybe he does—but that's the last thing dominating my mind and caressing my libido. Like every other woman in the room, my breaths are shallow and my pulse is triple its norm as he swaggers arrogantly on those custom ninja boots, his electric eyes gleaming behind that sleek Maserati mask.

Holy. Shit.

He's. Here. Out in a very public way—at a five-star resort that, as clearly as I can determine, isn't a hotbed for any hoodlums tonight, leading my brain to thunder with the same quandary Lydia just voiced. *What the hell* is *he doing here?*

Reece supplies the immediate answer as soon as his gaze locks on me. With a determined drop of his head, he marches directly through the crowd. *At me.* Somehow, I stay on my feet, barely subduing the giddy grin on my face, as he very nearly leaves piles of female tongues in his wake.

At last, he stops.

For at least a minute, we're silent. Stares tangling. Energies renewing. Connection reaffirmed.

Dear hell, I want to jump him. Worse than ever before. Will this feeling ever go away? Do I want it to?

He gives me the answer to that too, as soon as he scoops up my hand. The gloves are barely a shield for our heat, our need, our attraction.

*Deep breath. Deep breath.* The mantra is no use. My blood heats, all but dictating me to slam him to the wall and nail him right here. The wild sparks in the back of his gaze instantly reveal his exact same battle.

He clears his throat. And then again. And executes a low bow before brushing my knuckles with his lips, sending electrical zaps through all my fingers. He sneaks in a tiny bite to one. My heart turns over in my chest. Three times.

"Hi there, beauty."

Audible swoons ripple out from our bubble, spreading through the crowd like electrical pulses. Damn good comparison, in light of what he's doing to my whole nervous system.

"Hi there, gorgeous."

The murmur has barely left my lips when Mother and Father appear. The St. John dress is perfectly smoothed out. Father, from whom I got my light-blond hair, deep dimples, and round face, steps forward. He grabs Reece's hand, pumping it wildly, not letting go until the event photographer appears and snaps at least ten shots.

"Mr. Bolt," Father declares, milking the marketing op of a lifetime. "What an honor to have you here at our humble little event, sir. Are you a tennis fan?"

Reece nods. "I've dabbled. Though I'm more of a high-intensity thrill seeker."

Father throws back his head on a laugh. "Of *course* you are! Ha ha! Yes, yes."

Mother smoothly slips into the exchange. Her hands clasp demurely at her waist. Her smile is nearly a whitener commercial. "We must admit, this is quite a surprise. Any special reason for your appearance?" She gazes around, mouth dropping in mock horror. "Nobody here has been naughty tonight, have they?"

As the closest crowd members break out in laughter, Reece holds up a black-gloved hand. "You're all off the hook," he assures. "Well...everyone except her."

More stunned murmurs spread through the room. "Errmm... Emmalina?" Mother stutters, as if being told the coffee bar has run out of soy milk. "Really?"

"*Really.*" Reece shoots a look as if he wants to chuck the soy milk at her.

"Why?"

"Because I'm in love with her."

Heart melting.

Mother gawking.

Father glowing.

And boyfriend? Smirking. Robbing me of breath as his grin beams even wider—the moment he sweeps his free hand to the back of his head, fingers twisting at the clasp of his mask.

"I'm in love with her," he announces again. This time his face is exposed. "And I want the whole damn world to know it."

The air leaves the room.

No. Really.

"Hot damn," Father finally utters.

"Holy hell," Mother gasps.

"Oh, *sister!*" Lydia's exclamation is like a permission slip of reaction for the rest of the throng. Cell phone cameras are brandished, shouts are volleyed, and walls of humanity suddenly press in on us from every side. As sheer shock does the same thing to my heart, I grab Reece harder, stabbing the force of a thousand questions into my unblinking gape. In return, he palms my cheek with a gloved hand, his touch as tender as his kiss.

"It'll be all right, Velvet."

I twist a wry look. "Says who, hot stuff?"

He answers that by raising his hand into the air. At once, the room returns to silence, meaning my astounded gasp is an audible stab in the air. Even without the mask, the man brandishes special strength.

"Mr. and Mrs. Crist." My boyfriend, looking a dozen kinds of sexy with his thick, messy hair and leather-clad strength, pivots back toward my parents. "I'm here tonight, declaring this here, because your daughter is worth this. She's *my* super hero, and that's a truth the whole world needs to know." He draws a breath to follow up that but stops himself, shaking his head, before angling his gaze across the crowd. "You people see me doing all the flashy stuff, and you think I'm the noble one, the bold one, the badass against the bad guys." He chuffs, one side of his mouth ticking up. "But what I do is the easy game. Real heroes, those we should aspire to be, aren't made from roundhouse kicks or fancy fingertips that make light shows or dudes who can lob electric snowballs from time to time."

He faces me again. He steps in closer, bracing nearly toe-to-toe with me, consuming my vision with the utter beauty of his eyes, the loving lift of his lips.

"Heroes are people like all of us, who choose more for their lives and those of others, and are brave and bold and real about seeking those dreams." He still declares it in a raised voice, but it's one of the most intimate things he's ever said to me... One of his most meaningful gifts. "They don't accept anything less than living their truth and encouraging that bold, brutal honesty in others—like this amazing woman has done for me."

At that, the room erupts again—in a wild burst of applause.

I think.

There's not much I'm conscious of as tears blur my vision and joy rushes my heart, propelling me forward. Reece's mighty arms crush me closer, until our chests are pressed and our lips are meshed. "I love you," I tell him, once we can stand to pull apart by a few inches. All three syllables are drenched in the desire and amazement of my mind, my soul, my spirit.

"And I love you, Velvet." He dips in again, taking my mouth more gently.

"I know. *Wow*, do I know."

He grins while pulling me out of the ballroom, thanking Father for letting him "steal me away" as the lunch service begins. Before we go, I promise Lydia I'll return in time, with Reece in tow, to see her awards, but know I won't miss the meal one bit. What girl in their right mind has time for food when a hero in leather has just unmasked himself for her, in more ways than one, in front of two hundred people?

Once we find our way onto a walking path overlooking the ocean, Reece stops and spins me around, smashing me against him once more. Before I can say a word, his lips have descended, plunged, devoured, and dominated, tilting my balance and stealing my breath. Once I get my equilibrium back, I pull away a little, though maintain my hold with both hands deep in his hair. Doesn't look like the man minds one damn bit. He's full of seduction and adoration, wind-blown and sexy as hell.

And now someone's sucked the air out of *me,* too.

"So," he murmurs.

"So?" I tilt a coy grin.

"We *wow* worthy yet?"

I rear back to smack his shoulder but decide on a better torture—smashing my mouth back to his, parting his lips with my tongue, and not stopping until his crotch is hard and incessant against mine. When we're breathing hard and all but mauling each other on the path, I whisper against his lips, "*Wow.*"

"Good." He dips closer, cradling my hips in his powerful hold. Wind gusts over the bluff, carrying the sound of crashing waves and the electricity of the burgeoning night. "Because I want to give you a lifetime of wows, Emmalina."

Heart stopping, yet again.

And restarting at twice its speed, snagging my breath. "I want you in my life too."

His smile fades. He leans down, pressing his forehead to mine. "Even now?"

I grab both sides of his face and dig in my fingers, letting him know I understand the scope of the question. This is it. He's gone public—the super hero version of a handwritten invitation to all the globe's bad guys, not just The Consortium. He has no idea how easy he's just made my answer, given from every crevice of the heart he's filled.

"Yes, Mr. Richards. *Especially* now."

"Thank fuck." His exhale is a sexy growl as he gathers me close for another mind-bending kiss. As my thoughts fly and my blood heats, I release an eager sigh into his mouth—but attempt to compose my features once he lets me go. It's hard to chastise him when he looks this damn good, but I'm fixed on giving it my best shot.

"What took you so damn long?"

He snorts. "Three days?"

"Forever."

A wry nod. "Yeah. You're right. Forever." He nuzzles into my hair. "Fuck, I missed you."

"That's not an explanation."

"Right again, woman of mine." *Holy hell. Those words.* It's a struggle not to launch myself onto him once more, but I gulp hard, waiting for the follow-up brewing behind his stare. "I needed to take a beat. To recalibrate."

I laugh, biting my lip. "*That's* what you're calling this?"

He chuffs. "Why not?"

"Good point."

He takes another breath. "Before I came back to you, I just needed...to be sure."

"About what?"

"About all of it. The way I've been approaching this...super power." His brow furrows. "The way I've been approaching life."

I let a hand slide down to the middle of his chest. "You mean the life you were ready to chuck."

"Well, yes."

"Which was why you started going after criminals like a honey badger."

He's silent for a moment, caressing the curve of my waist, his fingers finally meeting at the small of my back. "I felt as freakish as a wild animal, so why not?"

I slowly shake my head. "But you made a very human decision. To make things better."

"Atonement," he volleys. "Hoping I'd tip the cosmic favor back my way a little bit—but that was before you came along and changed everything."

I attempt a laugh but it's stolen the moment his gaze, as silver as the stars yet as tender as the moonlight, pierces into me. "Hey." I lightly bat at his sternum. "You walked into *my* office, remember?"

He pulls me even closer, refitting our bodies together. "And from the moment I did, life wasn't the same." The wind, smelling of sea salt and night flowers, blows a chunk of his hair at the edge of his gaze. "Life was something I *wanted* again. And after you filled my heart, something I needed."

I circle my arms around his neck. "Reece." My whisper is paltry in the shadow of what he's given me, the enormity of the life he's made *me* need too. "God...Reece..."

"What is it, Velvet?"

"You're...my more."

"And you're my life." He utters it while sliding his lips within half a breath of mine, until I can feel the thunder of his heart and every electron in his bloodstream. But all too fast, his expression sobers. "This is really new territory for me, Emma."

I slide away, but only by a few inches. "Being an outted super hero?"

He slowly shakes his head. "Being in *love*."

My heart skips at least three beats. I lean on tiptoe to kiss his nose. "It's new territory for me too."

"We'll figure it out together." Our foreheads touch once more. "So let those fuckers come. We'll be ready."

I smile too—from all the jubilant depths of my heart. "We sure as hell will be."

He regards me with new concentration. "It's not going to be easy, Velvet. We don't live in a comic strip."

"I know." I pull on the back of his neck, taking his mouth in a long, adoring kiss. "But it'll be *life*."

He kisses me back. "It'll be together."

"It'll be more."

"It'll be us."

I swallow hard, swearing off the tears as his promise bursts to brilliance in my heart. As our lips meet again, a multitude of colors begin exploding in the sky. A synchronized laser show flashes up to join the fireworks.

It's beautiful. Electric. Chaotic. A little bit of insanity. A *lot* of intensity.

Just like our love.

The greatest super power of them all.

# MORE MISADVENTURES

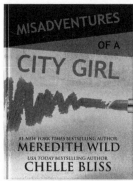

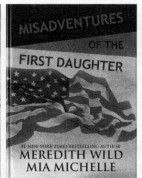

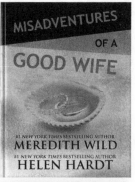

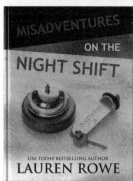

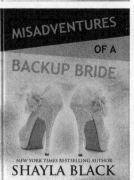

VISIT MISADVENTURES.COM
FOR MORE INFORMATION!

# ACKNOWLEDGMENTS

Where does a person start, when trying to wrap gray matter around the concept that their dream book has finally become a reality? I think the answer is that they just don't—and perhaps just try to stick to the singular overwhelming emotion at hand. *Gratitude.* A whole hell of a lot of it! I promise not to ramble on to the point they're "playing me off the stage," but I couldn't live with myself without thanking, from every corner of my heart and depth of my spirit, some incredible people who have helped Reece and Emma's story finally come to be.

*Meredith Wild and the Waterhouse Press Team: Jon, David, Shayla, Robyn*—for taking a chance on this cheesy little writer with big story ideas in her imagination. Your belief in the work has been so uplifting, overwhelming, and nonstop incredible, I continue to be utterly blown away. Thank you!

*Jeanne De Vita and Scott Saunders*—An editing team beyond compare! You have both worked so, so, *so* hard on this! Your love and passion for Reece and Emma's love story brings tears to my eyes. Soulfelt thanks to the two of you for holding my hand, calming my insecurities, and making the words sing. Your support has meant the world!

*Tracey Roelle*—Always my first set of eyes on everything! You've been by my side since the beginning and even dared to go where no human had ever been before: into the very first super hero idea I ever had! You could tell the world about that hideousness, but then I'd have to kill you...snicker.

*Victoria Blue*—Closest friend, sounding board, hand holder, and sanity maintainer! What a light you are in my life, and what a true super heroine you are to me, each and every day. I love you so much, chica!

*Shayla Black*—You were the first to encourage me to start writing again, and to indulge all my crazy ideas. Well, here's one of the craziest—and it never would have been possible without your steadfast belief. I'm so grateful, woman.

*Each and every member of the Payne Passion Force*—Your humor, support, jokes, laughter, and love keep me sane in special, beautiful ways. I love you ladies and gentlemen to the moon and truly appreciate you sharing your lives, loves, and passions on top of supporting the stories. It means more than you'll ever know!

# ABOUT ANGEL PAYNE

*USA Today* bestselling romance author Angel Payne has written for four publishing houses, and is also independently published. She loves to focus on high heat romance starring memorable alpha men and the women who love them.

She has numerous book series to her credit, including the Suited for Sin series, the Cimarron Saga, the Temptation Court series, the Secrets of Stone series (with Victoria Blue), the Lords of Sin historicals, and the popular WILD Boys of Special Forces series, as well as several stand-alone titles.

Currently, she is serving as the Vice President of Romance Writers of America's Passionate Ink Chapter. She lives in Southern California with her soul mate husband and beautiful daughter.

**VISIT HER AT ANGELPAYNE.COM!**